DREAMSCAPE

AN EROTIC FANTASY

JADE'S EROTIC ADVENTURES
BOOK 52

VICTORIA RUSH

VOLUME 52

JADE'S EROTIC ADVENTURES - BOOK 52

COPYRIGHT

ALSO BY VICTORIA RUSH

Adult Fairytales:

The Enchanted Forest: An Erotic Fairytale

The Land of Giants: An Erotic Fairytale

The Dragon's Lair: An Erotic Fairytale

Witch's Brew: An Erotic Fairytale

The Mage's Spell: An Erotic Fairytale

The Mermaid Lagoon: An Erotic Fairytale

The Coven: An Erotic Fairytale

Rapunzel: An Erotic Fairytale

The Seven Dwarfs: An Erotic Fairytale

The Land of Mutants: An Erotic Fairytale

The Erotic Temple: A Sexy Fairytale (Coming Soon)

Erotica Themed Bundles:

Voyeur: Lesbian Erotica Bundle

Public Affairs: A Lesbian Anthology

Futa Fantasies: The Ladyboy Collection

Threesomes: The Lesbian Collection

Threesomes - Volume 2: The Lesbian Collection

First Time: A Lesbian Anthology

Hedonism: An Erotic Anthology

Switch Hitters: Bisexual Erotica

Taboo Erotica: The Lesbian Series

BDSM: The Lesbian Collection

Party Games: The Erotic Collection

Party Games 2: The Erotic Collection

All Girl 1: Lesbian Erotica Bundle

All Girl 2: Lesbian Erotica Bundle

All Girl 3: Lesbian Erotica Bundle

All Girl 4: Lesbian Erotica Bundle

Erotic Fairytale Bundles:

Clover's Fantasy Adventures: Books 1 - 5

Clover's Fantasy Adventures: Books 6 - 10

Erotic Fantasy:

Pirate's Bounty: A Time Travel Adventure

Wild West: A Time Travel Adventure

Private Riley: A Time Travel Adventure

Cleopatra's Secret: A Time Travel Adventure

Bounty Hunter 2125: A Time Travel Adventure

Ninja Assassin: A Time Travel Adventure

The 300: A Time Travel Adventure

Arabian Nights: An Erotic Fairytale (coming soon...)

Steamy Time Travel Bundles:

Riley's Time Travel Adventures: Books 1 - 5

Lesbian Erotica:

The Dinner Party: Lesbian Voyeur Erotica

The Darkroom: Bisexual Voyeur Erotica

Naked Yoga: Lesbian Transgender Erotica

Nude Cruise: Bisexual Voyeur Erotica

Rush Hour: Taboo Public Sex

The Girl Next Door: First Time Lesbian Erotic Romance

Girls' Camp: Lesbian Group Sex

Wet Dream: Ladyboy Fantasy Erotica

The Convent: Taboo Sex with a Nun

Sex Robot: A Dream Sex Machine

The Personal Trainer: Getting Pumped at the Gym

The Dominatrix: BDSM Lesbian Domination

Webcam Chat: Lesbian Online Sex

Paint Me: A Kinky Bodypainting Workshop

The Toy Party: Girls Sharing Sex Toys

The Costume Party: Strapping One On

Swedish Sauna: Lesbian Group Sex

The Therapist: Taboo Lesbian Erotica

Elevator Shaft: Bisexual Threesomes Erotica

Ladyboy: Lesbian Transgender Erotica

Peep Show: Lesbian Voyeur Erotica

The Dare: Public Sex Erotica

Maid Service: Lesbian Threesomes Erotica

The Hitchhiker: First Time Lesbian Erotica

The Housesitter: Spycam Lesbian Erotica

The Spa: Lesbian Group Orgy

Parlor Games: Blindfold Sex Party

The Exchange Student: First Time Lesbian Erotica

The Hostel: Bisexual Group Erotica

The Harem: Lesbian Erotic Romance

The Orient Express: Lesbian Voyeur Erotica

The First Lady: A Forbidden Lesbian Erotic Romance

The Slave: Lesbian BDSM Erotica

The Masseuse: Lesbian Sensuous Erotica

Too Close for Comfort: Lesbian Forbidden Erotica

Naked Twister: A Wild Party Game

Lexi: The Sex App (Lesbian Fantasy Erotica)

Call Girl: Lesbian Bisexual Threesomes Erotica

Circle Jill: Lesbian Masturbation Workshop

The Viewing Room: Masturbation Voyeur Erotica

Spin the Bottle: A Kinky Party Game

The Hair Salon: Lesbian Voyeur Erotica

Tribadism 1: Girls Only Sex Workshop

Tribadism 2: The Art of Scissoring

Tribadism 3: Threeway Hookups

The Kiss: A Game of Oral Sex

Pledge Week: Sorority Sisters

Carny Games 1: A Wild Sex Party

Carny Games 2: A Kinky Sex Party

Carny Games 3: An Erotic Sex Party

Dreamscape: An Artificial Reality Game

Glory Hole: Guess Who's On the Other Side

Joy Ride: A Late Night Erotic Bus Trip

The Blind Girl: An Erotic Romance(Coming Soon)

Lesbian Erotica Bundles:

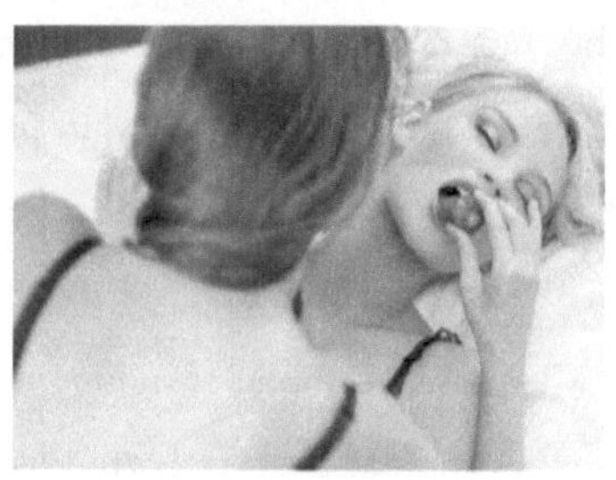

Jade's Erotic Adventures: Books 1 - 5

Jade's Erotic Adventures: Books 6 - 10

Jade's Erotic Adventures: Books 11 - 15

Jade's Erotic Adventures: Books 16 - 20

Jade's Erotic Adventures: Books 21 - 25

Jade's Erotic Adventures: Books 26 - 30

Jade's Erotic Adventures: Books 31 - 35

Jade's Erotic Adventures: Books 36 - 40

Jade's Erotic Adventures: Books 41 - 45

Jade's Erotic Adventures: Books 46 - 50

Fifty Shades of Jade: Superbundle

Standalone Stories:

The Polynesian Girl: A Lesbian EroticRomance

For the uninhibited...

WANT TO AMP UP YOUR SEX LIFE?

Sign up for my newsletter to receive more free books and other steamy stuff. Discover a hundred different ways to wet your whistle!

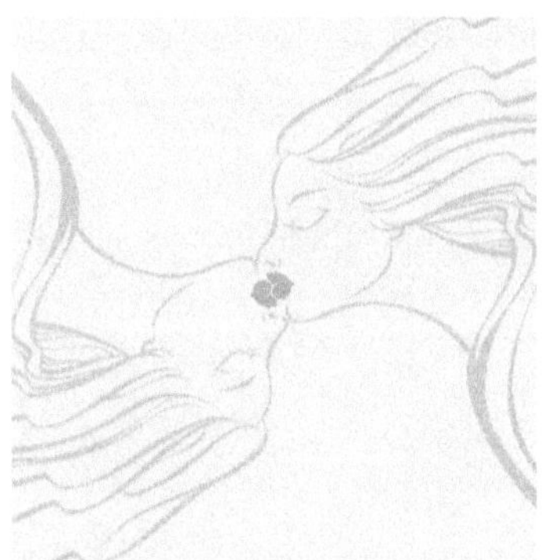

Victoria Rush Erotica

1

___

I noticed the sign out of the corner of my eye while driving to the mall. Eros – The Virtual Reality Fantasy Club. The tagline read *Live out your wildest dreams in the privacy of your own room*. With flashing red and yellow lights circulating around the billboard, it was pretty hard to miss. I slowed at a nearby stoplight and glanced at the storefront, squinting my eyes at the frosted glass windows. It was impossible to see anything inside beyond some moving shadows, and I shook my head, wondering what kind of operation they were running.

I'd heard of virtual reality, of course. A computer-generated simulation of a realistic environment where you wore special goggles or equipment to focus your attention. But why the frosted glass on the windows? What were they trying to hide? It almost seemed like one of those adult stores where they papered over the windows to protect everyone's identity. And what did they mean by living out your wildest dreams? Was this some kind of fantasy sex club?

The more I thought about it, the more intrigued I

became. I enjoyed using sex toys and porn videos to simulate sex with imaginary partners, but I was always conscious that I was alone and self-directing my pleasure. The idea of being in a private room with state-of-the-art technology to lose myself in the ultimate fantasy would take my erotic role-playing to an entirely new level. I decided to circle back to the club on my return from the mall to look into it further.

But after becoming increasingly distracted while shopping for new clothes, I decided to cut my mall visit short and rushed back to the club, feeling a growing wet spot in my panties. I parked my car a block away from the storefront, then I scurried up to the front door, hoping none of my friends or work colleagues would recognize me. When I opened the door, I saw a tastefully appointed reception area with modern leather armchairs and a pretty receptionist sitting behind a curved desk.

"May I help you?" she said when she noticed me peering at the movie-style posters lining the wall, depicting various fantasy scenes.

"Um, yes..." I stammered. "I just noticed your sign and wondered how this works exactly. I've never experienced something like this before–"

"One of our customer service agents will be with you shortly, if you'd like to have a seat," the girl said, motioning to one of the chairs. "May I have your name?"

"Jade," I said, taking a seat in the empty reception area, wondering what I'd gotten myself into.

The fact that there were no visible sign of customers made me wonder if this operation was legit. But the posters on the wall seemed professionally made and beautifully rendered, with gorgeous models posing in different settings ranging from science fiction to fantasy to exotic tropical islands. I didn't recognize any of the models, and I wasn't even sure if they were real people or just super-realistic CGI illustrations. But one thing was for certain. The images they depicted were highly stimulating and real enough to make me squirm in my seat while I imagined myself in one or more of the scenarios. If the live, 3-D versions of these characters and settings were anything like the two-dimensional poster illustrations, then I was definitely interested in exploring it further.

"Jade?" a pretty woman wearing a form-fitting business suit said, approaching my chair.

"Yes," I said, turning my head in surprise while I snapped out of my daydream.

"I understand you'd like some more information about our services," the woman said. "Would you like to accompany me to my office where we can talk in private?"

"Sure," I said, standing up and darting my eyes over her sexy figure.

"My name's Jillian," the woman said, extending her hand toward me.

"Pleased to meet you," I said, feeling my cheeks flushing while I gazed at her piercing blue eyes and plump lips.

"I'm down this way," Jillian said, extending her hand and leading me down a narrow hall lined with closed doors.

While I followed close behind, staring at her tight, round ass, I heard the sound of muffled moans and voices coming from behind some of the doors, and I wondered if there was more than one person involved in these role-playing scenarios.

Jillian led me into her office, then she invited me to sit in one of the two chairs on the opposite side of her desk.

"May I get you something to drink?" she said. "Coffee or tea perhaps?"

"I'm fine, thank you," I said, not entirely sure I'd be able to hold a cup of hot fluid without spilling it from my already trembling hands.

After I was seated, she sat in the chair beside me instead of behind her desk, then she crossed her leg over her knee, displaying her slender and toned muscles. I couldn't help stealing a glance at her sexy thighs, feeling my heart pounding in my chest while I gripped the handles of my chair firmly. I wasn't sure if my heightened reaction had more to do with the strange environment I found myself in or Jillian's movie-star looks. Either way, I was already primed and super-aroused, with my burning clit rubbing against the seam of my jeans and my panties soaked all the way through.

"Is this your first experience with virtual reality?" Jillian said, crossing her hands gently in her lap.

"Yes," I chuckled nervously. "Unless you count watching porn and playing with sex toys."

"Well, if *that's* the kind of scenarios you like to fantasize about," she said. "I can assure you that the imagery and equipment we use at our facility is nothing like anything you've ever tried before."

"How does it work, exactly?" I said, pinching my eyebrows. "Is it just fancy headphones and goggles that show 3-D movies?"

"Oh, it's much more than that," Jillian smiled. "For starters, you'll wear a full-body suit and a special helmet with sensors to stimulate all of your senses. Plus, you sit in an animatronic chair that swivels and shakes to mimic the sensation of being in a moving environment."

"You mean like those flight training simulators that pilots use?"

"Yes, except these simulators are also equipped with special probes and sensors to provide two-way feedback."

"What kind of two-way feedback?"

"The kind that enables you to experience your interaction with the characters in your selected scenes as if you were really there."

"Are you referring to my sense of *touch*?" I said, beginning to understand what she was getting at.

"And taste and smell..." she nodded.

"How is that even possible?" I said, widening my eyes in surprise.

"Like I said," Jillian smiled. "We have extremely sophisticated and sensitive equipment. I think you'll find it stimulates your passions in ways you can only imagine."

"And these *scenarios* you mentioned earlier," I said, feeling the wet spot in my jeans growing larger by the moment. "Do you have a fairly broad range to choose from?"

"We have over a hundred different settings and scenarios you can select, from expensive nightclubs to tropical islands to sensuous spas. Just about anywhere you've dreamed about going, we've recreated in a full, sensory experience."

"And what about the *characters* I choose to interact with? Can I select those as well?"

"Of course," Jillian nodded. "You can choose the age, gender, sexual persuasion, and body type of the main characters, as you prefer. And even mix them up from one scene to the next."

"Really?" I said, becoming increasingly intrigued by Jillian's description. "Are these scenes *pre-programmed* like a movie, where I'm just passively watching and experiencing the action while seated in the chair?"

"That's the beauty of our VR program," Jillian grinned. "It's entirely customized to your experience, reacting in real time to your vocalizations and bodily responses, just as you would with a real person."

"How do you do that?" I said, shaking my head in disbelief.

"Everything is driven by our artificial intelligence engine. It responds to your actions in the normal manner, through both vocal and physical responses. At least as *normal* as you can imagine from the opulent world you choose to implant yourself in and the sexy characters you choose to surround yourself with."

"Wow," I said, squirming in my seat while I imagined myself in these fantasy scenarios. "And these *physical responses* that I'll receive, are they also super-realistic and similar to real-life settings?"

"As close as you can imagine to the real thing," Jillian smiled. "Would you like me to take you to one of the private rooms for you to sample one for yourself?"

"Yes, if it's not too much trouble," I nodded, feeling my ass sticking to the seat of her chair.

2

———

J illian swiveled her desktop monitor toward her side of the desk, then she tapped on the keyboard, pulling up a floorplan of the facility that showed which rooms were in use and which ones were currently free.

"Alright," she said, standing up and holding out her hand to help me up. "It looks like we've got room 8B open for the next hour or so. Would you like to come with me?"

"Yes, please," I smiled, peering down at the wet stain between my legs, wondering if she knew exactly how literally I wanted to accept her invitation.

While we walked down the narrow hallway toward the room at the end of the hall, I listened to the sound of soft moans and panting coming from the other side of the doors from both men and women. By now, it seemed obvious exactly what kind of scenarios most of the club's patrons chose to fantasy play with, and by the time we reached our appointed room, I was ready to tear off Jillian's clothes and slam the door behind us while I ravished her body.

Instead, I glanced at a heavily padded, plastic-lined

lounge chair that looked like one of those full-body massagers, except this one was attached to a steel platform with hydraulic pistons and switches. On opposite sides of the room hung two bodysuits with glass helmets that reminded me of the astronaut suits the moon-landers wore.

"That's quite an apparatus," I said, peering at the chair with squinted eyes.

"You have *no* idea," Jillian grinned, motioning for me to take a seat. "Why don't you try it on for size?"

"Will this be a full simulation?" I said, glancing at her erect nipples darting the thin fabric of her silk blouse.

"Not unless you're ready to book a full hour. This will just be a brief demonstration of some of its features."

"Okay..." I said, lying down in the chair cautiously.

Jill picked up a remote control device from beside the apparatus, then she tapped a few buttons and the chair began to rock forward and back gently, not unlike the fucking action of a male partner lying on top of me.

"That's a familiar feeling," I nodded, smiling up at her. "It's too bad this thing doesn't come equipped with some *other* equipment like a real person–"

"You mean something like *this*?" she said, twisting one of the knobs on the remote control.

Suddenly, a super-realistic, penis-shaped dildo slid up from a hidden crease in the seat, flaring into the gap between my stained jeans. I couldn't help reaching down to touch the object while I compared it to some of the other sex toys I used at home. This one felt more flexible and realistic to the touch, even swelling subtly when I caressed the tip of the animatronic erection.

"Holy shit," I panted. "This is as close to the real thing as I've ever felt with a simulated sex toy. What *other* surprises does this chair have?"

"You'll have to book a session to find out," Jillian said. "But I can assure you that it has capabilities far beyond what a real person can do. And that doesn't even take into consideration all the other probes and sensors contained within the bodysuit that you'll be wearing while you're strapped into the chair."

"Am I supposed to climb into it completely *naked*?" I said, peering up at the suit on the wall.

"It's certainly more fun that way," Jillian said. "That is, if you want to experience the full range of sensations in the most realistic manner. It's kind of like the difference between having sex with a condom versus without one."

"What about *hygiene*?" I said, running my hand over the clear plastic cover of the lounge chair. "I imagine people emit all kinds of bodily fluids while strapped into this getup. How do you keep people from spreading sexually transmitted diseases?"

"The seats and suits receive a high-pressure, antiseptic steam wash after every finished session," Jillian nodded. "It's actually a cleaner environment than your own freshly laundered bed."

I paused for a moment while I softly rubbed the seam of my jeans against the faux hard-on.

"I'm definitely willing to give it a try if this room is available," I nodded. "How much does it cost?"

"Fifty dollars for a twenty-minute trial, then one hundred dollars for every hour you choose afterward. But this room is booked for another client in a couple of hours, and we need an hour turnaround time to clean the equipment, so you can try it out for the first hour if you'd like."

"Let's start with the twenty-minute trial, then I'll extend the session for the full hour if I like it. Where do I sign up?"

"You can fill out the necessary paperwork with Annie at

the front desk and she'll take your credit card deposit. Then come back to see me, and I'll give you instructions for getting started."

Oh, I'll come alright, I thought to myself while I ran my eyes over Jillian's sexy figure. *I'll come all over your pretty face while I imagine you licking me on this machine.*

3

———

After I completed the registration information at the front desk, I returned to Jillian's office, where she gave me the instructions for starting the first session.

"So what happens now?" I said, already shaking in excitement.

"It's pretty simple," she nodded. "You go into your private booth and put on the suit and helmet, then sit in the chair and press the start button."

"I noticed there were two suits in the room. Does it matter which one I use?"

"Yes, one is for men and the other is for women. You'll notice some subtle differences in the design. The men's suit is slightly larger and has a bigger crotch area to accommodate the extra stimulation equipment. But they're also clearly marked, so you shouldn't have any difficulty figuring out which one to use."

"How do I choose the scenarios in which I wish to engage after I press the start button?"

"Everything is controlled by voice commands. A pop-up

menu will appear on your helmet visor, where you can select each of the elements of your scene. Once the scene begins, you simply talk to the characters you encounter and everything will pretty much play out the way you desire."

"What if I need some help?"

"I think you'll find everything is very user-friendly and intuitive. In the unlikely event that you run into a snag, just say the words *VR Help* and the scene will pause while an automated agent responds to your query."

"How will I know how much time I've got left?"

"There's a small countdown timer on the lower-right-hand corner of the screen that shows you how much time you have remaining in your scheduled session."

"Sounds good," I nodded. "I think I'm ready to go. Wish me luck."

"Luck won't have anything to do with it," Jillian smiled. "Once you enter the VR world, your destiny is entirely within your grasp. And I suspect it will exceed your expectations."

"Okay," I said, peering at her exposed cleavage, wanting to grasp something else. "Thanks for your help."

When I got into my private room and latched the door behind me, I walked up to the nearest wall and gazed at the suit hanging on a hook. A patch in the center of the chest displayed a male gender symbol, and I glanced down to the crotch area of the suit, noticing a slight bulge and a different type of covering. I couldn't help touching it with my palm, feeling a spongy material overlaid with a stretchy fabric, and I smiled. If the chair had embedded a natural-feeling erect cock for *women* to play with, then it seemed obvious that the men's suit would have an equally adaptable accessory embedded within it to simulate the feel of a woman's pussy.

Or *mouth*.

I walked over to the opposite wall and pulled the women's suit off the hook, then I unzipped the front of it, feeling the groin area for any kind of attachments. There was a spongy, oblong disc with a small slit positioned over the area corresponding to the front of my mound, and suddenly my panties began to moisten at the thought of what the device could do. Then I slid my fingers a little lower in the crotch area, feeling a hole in the suit, and I nodded, remembering how Jillian had made the artificial cock pop up from the chair.

"Jesus," I panted, tearing off my clothes and slowly climbing into the suit.

It felt warm and rubbery, almost like a neoprene wetsuit, but there were small electrodes and nodules centered over my key erogenous zones, and I could already feel the skin over my entire body beginning to tingle at the thought of what awaited me. I lifted the glass helmet off the shelf next to the hook and placed it gently over my head, happy to find that it had large ventilation slits next to my nose and my mouth to make it easy to breathe. The area over my eyes was encased in clear glass, making it possible to view my external surroundings, but the area around my mouth had a spongy layer not unlike what I saw in the crotch of the men's suit.

"Alright," I said, turning the bottom of my helmet to secure it to the top part of my suit. "Let's get this party started."

I lay down in the reclining chair and tapped the Start button on the right hand rest, then an illuminated display appeared on the glass visor directly in front of my eyes. The menu began by asking me to choose what kind of setting I wished to engage with, and after scrolling down the list by shifting the direction of my gaze, I decided on a nightclub scene by voicing the word *Nightclub*.

Cool, I nodded to myself, happy to see how easy it was to navigate the system.

The next menu item asked me to choose what gender and sexual preference I wanted for my primary character interaction, and after some hesitation, I choose *male-hetero-sexual*. There'd be plenty of chances to have some fun with the women and transgender choices at another time, but for this first session, I was eager to find out what the special dildo in the seat cushion was programmed to do.

The final menu choice asked me to select the body type, race, hair color, and age of my primary character interaction. It took a little longer to review all the options before deciding on a plain vanilla, thirty-five-year-old, brown-haired white male model with a swimmer's build. When the AI engine popped up a three-dimensional image of my selected model, naked from the waist up, I nodded my head and said *'Yes, please.'*

I was a little disappointed that the menu didn't also give me the option to choose the *penis* size of my model, but I figured that might have something to do with the nature of the scenario each player chose to run. It was possible that not every client wanted a sex simulation, and besides, part of the fun would be learning what hidden features might reveal themselves based on my prompts and commands.

A few seconds later, the screen changed to reveal a dimly lit nightclub setting showing a mixed group of twenty- and thirty-year-old strangers milling around an open lounge and flashing dance floor. The cinematography looked like something straight out of a movie, except everything was rendered in 3-D, making it look like an authentic real-world setting, including the characters, which were virtually indistinguishable from real people. I turned my head to pan around the room, and the image automatically adjusted to focus on the area I wanted to see. I noticed the familiar features of the model I'd chosen from the start menu sitting alone at the bar, and I slowly approached the counter while running my eyes over his muscular physique clad in a tight button-up shirt and dark jeans.

"Looks like you could use some company," I said, pausing by his chair, trying not to roll my eyes at my lame pickup line.

"I was just thinking the same thing," he smiled, motioning for me to join him on the adjacent empty stool.

"Oh?" I said, peering at his reflection in the smoky mirror behind the bar. "Were you checking me out?"

"Just noticing that you seemed a little *lost*," he nodded. "First time at the Copacabana?"

"I suppose you could say that," I chuckled. "This is a first for me in more ways than one."

"You mean nightclubs aren't your usual scene?" he said, darting his eyes over my face and my bare shoulders.

The AI system had automatically dressed my doppelgänger in a scene-appropriate outfit, choosing a tasteful but tight-fitting, black silk dress, cropped mid-thigh. I glanced in the bar mirror and flared my eyes at how accurately the system had reproduced my facial features and body shape. If I didn't know that I was already cocooned in a strange VR bodysuit, I would never have known that the image I saw of myself in the reflection wasn't the real me wearing a different outfit.

"Can I get you something to drink?" the man said, noticing me peering toward the glass bottles lined up on the shelf at the back of the bar.

"Oh, yes," I said, pulling out of my trance. "I'll have a dirty martini, thanks."

The man motioned for the bartender and ordered two martinis, then he swiveled his chair toward me, spreading his legs slightly apart to accommodate my knees protruding over the edge of the stool.

"I'm Alec," he said, extending his hand softly over the counter toward me.

"Jade," I said, clasping his hand with my gloved hand, surprised to see how natural his warm skin felt in my palm.

It took every ounce of my willpower not to steal a glance between his parted legs to get a preview of his package, but for some strange reason, I kept my focus where it properly belonged during our first meeting, even though I knew the entire scene was staged and that I could do whatever I wanted with my simulated character with total impunity.

"I like that name," Alec smiled, darting his eyes over my face. "It matches your pretty eyes."

"I bet you use that line on *all* the girls you meet in this place," I laughed, beginning to wonder just how natural and adaptable the artificial intelligence engine was with speech recognition.

"Only the *pretty* ones," he said. "I haven't had a chance to use it for quite some time now."

"No?" I said. "Nightclubs aren't your usual scene either?"

"It's not that," he said. "It's just that I haven't seen anyone quite so intriguing as you in a long time."

"Do tell," I smiled, angling my seat more in his direction and brushing the inside of his thigh with my crossed legs. "You know how a woman always likes to be flattered."

"You mean besides your impossibly long and shapely *legs*?" he said, glancing down toward my thighs. "It's something about your countenance. You don't seem like so many of other girls that wear too much makeup and too-tight dresses. They have a smell of desperation about them."

"I thought that's what most men *wanted*?" I teased. "Scantily clad women who wear their intentions on their sleeve."

"There's something to be said for the art of subtlety," Alec said. "I find the dance of courtship much more interesting than the capturing of the prize."

"Well said, my friend," I smiled, raising my glass and taking a sip of my martini.

"To *friendship*," he said, lifting his glass and softly clinking it against mine.

I peered into his hazel eyes while he sipped his cocktail, flashing my gaze over his handsome face. With his chiseled cheekbones, square jaw, and perfectly straight nose, he looked like something straight out of a cologne commercial. In fact, I could sense his musky scent wafting over my nose, and I twitched it unconsciously, surprised that the VR system was able to replicate so many of the senses I took for granted in the real world.

"Is everything okay with your drink?" Alec said, noticing my facial twitch.

"Definitely," I said. "It's more than okay. I was just savoring the taste and the smell–"

"Of your *martini*?" he said.

"Among other things," I smiled, separating my legs and crossing them over slowly in the other direction.

"Hmm," he nodded, sliding his right palm over the counter toward me. "I was just thinking the same thing."

"About your *cocktail*?" I said.

"Among other things..."

"Mmm," I said, feeling the tips of my fingers tingling when he touched me. "Is there somewhere else we can go for a little privacy? I'd kind of like to taste something *else* right about now."

"There's a private room in the back where we can get more comfortable if you'd like," he said, tilting his head toward a closed-off section of the nightclub.

"I'd like that," I nodded. "That is, if you think we're not rushing too quickly to the prize."

"I can't imagine what you're referring to," he grinned, holding out his hand to help me off the stool. "But so far, this courtship has aroused much more than just my passing interest."

"Mmm, so I can see," I said, peering down at his bulging crotch.

While he slowly led me through the teeming crowd of nightclub patrons, I felt my suit beginning to tighten around my pussy while I dribbled a stream of juices down the inside of my thigh.

This should be interesting, I thought, unconsciously clasping his hand tighter while I imagined what was going to happen next.

4

———

Alec led me to a closed door guarded by a burly bouncer, then he passed the man a crisp one-hundred-dollar bill, and the guard opened the door, motioning for us to go inside. The room was dimly lit with a large sectional sofa and a few armchairs with small side tables to hold drinks, but otherwise had few decorations to indicate its purpose. With no windows and only one exit door, in any other situation I might be reluctant to enter such a vulnerable space with a stranger, but I kept reminding myself this was just a fantasy.

"You seem to know your way around this place," I said, circling my arms around his neck and pressing my hips against his groin.

"It has its advantages," he nodded, kissing me softly while he traced a finger up the small of my back.

I could feel his moist lips on my mouth and I hesitated, knowing I was kissing a robotic device implanted inside my helmet, but it felt so realistic that I unconsciously slipped my tongue into his cavity and closed my eyes, losing myself in the moment. While he rolled his tongue softly against mine, he drew his hand a few inches further up my back, slowly pulling down my zipper. I groaned in his mouth, and he pinched the fingers of one hand over my bra clasp, deftly unfastening it in one motion before sliding his palms down the sides of my exposed torso.

"I wish *every* man I met was as skilled as you," I purred, pulling back a few inches to peer into his smoldering eyes.

"I've had a little practice," he smiled.

"Maybe somebody just *taught* you well," I said, knowing his responses were entirely driven by a sophisticated computer program.

But at this point it hardly mattered, with my pussy leaking like a faucet and my nipples hard as forty-five-caliber bullets.

"Like I said earlier," he said, pinching my teats softly and twisting them between his fingers while my dress slipped down over my hips onto the floor. "Most of the fun is in the playing of the game, not winning the contest. Every partner brings their own talents to the table, and I have to adapt to their strategies in order to reach the goal."

"And what's the goal in this case?" I said.

"Making you *happy*, of course," he grinned, sliding his hands down the front of my trembling stomach.

"What about *you*?" I said, pushing him gently away while I began unbuttoning his shirt. "Is there any room for pleasure on *your* side of the scrimmage line?"

"I suppose that depends on how *talented* my opponent is," he said, pressing his hips forward when I reached his belt.

I gazed into his eyes while I unclasped his belt, then I unbuttoned the top of his trousers and began to pull his zipper down when some lights suddenly started flashing in the lower-right-hand corner of my visor, warning me that I only had a few seconds remaining in my scheduled session.

"Wait, what?" I said. "No–"

"Are you having second thoughts?" Alec said, peering up at me with a wrinkled forehead. "Maybe we're going too fast–"

"No, it's not that," I stammered, trying to remember Jillian's codeword for getting support.

Then the screen suddenly went blank, and I shook my head, cursing.

"Fuck!" I huffed. "Could this happen at a worse possible time? Help! Help!"

But the screen remained unresponsive, and I almost pulled off my helmet in frustration while my breath began to fog up the visor. Then I suddenly remembered the codeword Jillian had given me if I ran into a glitch, and I nodded my head, feeling my heart pounding in my chest.

"VR Help, VR Help," I shouted, feeling the streams of lubrication beginning to run down the inside of my thighs.

"Yes, Jade," a soft robotic voice purred into my ears. "How can I help you?"

"I want to continue my session," I said, still breathing heavily. "Can you extend my session for the remaining hour?"

"Of course," the robot voice said. "Do you wish to continue the previous scene where you left off, or start a new one?"

"Where I left off, please," I panted.

"No problem. Please stand by."

After a couple of seconds, the familiar setting of the nightclub room came back into view, with Alec standing half-dressed in front of me, displaying a puzzled expression.

"Is everything alright?" he said, placing his hand on my exposed shoulder and squeezing it gently.

"Yes," I said. "Sorry, I just had a little moment of distraction. Can we pick up where we left off?"

"Of course," he said, sliding his hands down the sides of my bare arms and gently clasping my hands as he stepped toward me, kissing me softly while we crossed our arms over each other's chests.

"I believe I was about to ease your *discomfort*," I smiled, reaching down and pulling his unzipped trousers over his hips while I peered at his swelling erection straining against his tight boxer-briefs.

I bent my knees and slowly began kissing my way down his muscular chest, feeling the undulations of his rippling six-pack with the tip of my nose, then I knelt down between his legs, slipping my fingers under his waistband and pulling his briefs over his organ. When it popped up and slapped me on the side of my face, I gasped at how large and beautiful it was. Perfectly straight, with a light-brown caramel color, his circumcised crown flared while I stared at his slit, emitting a light drop of dew.

I placed the tips of my fingers on each side of his thick shaft and traced them slowly toward his tightening sac, watching his phallus flexing in front of my face.

"Where've you *been* all my life?" I said, leaning forward and licking the underside of his flagstaff toward his dripping glans.

"Waiting for *you*, apparently," he groaned when I encircled his glans with my watering mouth and slid my tongue under the heart-shaped crease. "I take back what I said earlier. Sometimes the prize can be just as rewarding as the chase."

"Mm-hmm," I smiled, gripping his hard tool in both

hands and bobbing my head up and down over his burning bulb.

I would have been more than happy to finish him with my mouth with the short amount of time I had remaining, but as he ran his fingers softly through my hair while I sucked on his throbbing erection, he lowered his hands under my chin and slowly extracted his manhood from my eager mouth.

"You're going to expend all my energy if you keep sucking me like that," he said. "And I'm not ready for this game to be over before *you* score a few runs also."

"I can't imagine what you mean," I grinned, slowly straightening up and wiping off the drool running down the side of my chin with the back of my hand.

"Let's see if we can put this instrument to better use," he said, placing his hands over the back of my ass and raising me up in one swift motion, aiming the tip of his prick toward my dripping hole.

"Fuck yes," I murmured, wrapping my legs around his hips while he entered my slit with his big organ.

"Oh God..." I groaned, feeling his girth stretching me apart until he filled my entire cavity like a torpedo in a tight submarine tube.

As he began to rock his hips slowly against my splayed legs, I pulled my face closer to his and thrust my tongue deep into his mouth, feeling his flexing chest muscles rubbing against my swinging tits. He barely seemed to be working up a sweat while he held me like a rag doll, slapping his thick organ against my pussy while we moaned in each other's mouth. I knew it was just a fantasy and that no ordinary man would be able to fuck me like this for very long, but I savored every moment as I watched the countdown timer slowly counting down toward the end of my scheduled session.

I came two times while he expertly fucked me, tilting my body at the precise angle to rub my burning clit against the top of his erection while he waited patiently for me to satisfy my cravings before he considered seeking his own pleasure. After my second orgasm, I glanced at the flashing clock, noticing we had only a few minutes left before time ran out, and I pulled my head back to peer at his dilated pupils.

"I think it's time for *you* to score a run now," I smiled. "I'm already ahead two-to-nothing. You don't want to finish the game with a *shutout*, do you?"

"That would be a blemish on my record," he grinned, squeezing my buttocks harder while stretching my dripping labia over his hard balls. "You better get ready though, because I'm about to hit a home run."

"Fire when ready," I nodded, squeezing my legs harder around his hips. "I might have one more in me if you swing your bat hard enough."

"Mm-hmm," Alec grunted, kissing me passionately on my lips while he plowed his dick even deeper inside me.

While I listened to the sound of his escalating panting and moans, I could feel the pressure inside me building in lockstep with him toward a powerful climax. When it finally washed over me like a tidal wave, I gushed my juices hard over his balls, feeling his cock pulsating inside me like a fire-hose. We both shook and convulsed against one another for what seemed like an eternity, then the screen suddenly went blank again as I panted inside my helmet, suddenly aware of my position in the mechanical chair. I peered down, noticing that I was gripping the hand rests tightly with both arms, and my legs elevated high in the air with crossed ankles while the huge brown dildo dripped softly between my glistening gash.

"Holy shit," I panted out loud. "I have *got* to come back to this place for more of this stuff. Talk about a *grand slam*. That was quite possibly the best sex I've ever had."

5

____

I couldn't book another VR session for almost a week because the place was so busy, but in the meantime I scrolled through their website, browsing the long list of fantasy scenarios from their menu. From expensive spas to tropical getaways to luxury cruises, the list seemed almost endless. This time, I didn't want to take any chance at getting cut off in the middle of a steamy session, so I booked a two-hour appointment when one opened up, hoping to sample at least two different scenes.

While I flashed back to the hot simulation with Alec in the nightclub, I stood in front of my bathroom mirror with one leg propped up on the counter, imagining him fucking me with his big cock while I plowed three fingers into my pussy. I imagined it was him I was looking at instead of me, with his strong arms cradling my ass while I quivered and came all over my hands. By the time my next scheduled session at the VR club rolled around, I was already at a fever pitch of excitement, anticipating who I would encounter next.

After sticking my head into Jillian's office and asking for

a suggestion for an all-girl hookup this time, she recommended I try the 'nude cruise' episode. When I got into my appointed room, I quickly donned my stretchy spacesuit and sat in the reclining chair, pressing the start button. The LED menu popped up on the visor, and I togged through the familiar list, choosing my preferences. For the Setting, I scrolled until I found the Nude Cruise option, then for gender and sexual preference, I chose female/lesbian before changing it to female/bisexual. If there might be an opportunity for a mixed threesome somewhere in the mix, I wouldn't turn that down.

When the next menu item asked me to select the body type, race, hair color, and age for my primary character interaction, I chose a curvy Latina, brown-haired, thirty-five-year-old, hoping for a meeting with a Jennifer Lopez lookalike. But when the view suddenly flashed to the top deck of a luxury cruise ship sailing through the tranquil waters of the Caribbean, my eyes widened watching the figures of the beautiful passengers strolling past me. Every one of them was stark naked, with gorgeous, buff physiques and matinee-idol looks. I could already feel my pussy throbbing while I gawked at the spectacle, and suddenly, I felt weak in my knees. I peered around and noticed a few vacant lounge chairs next to the deckside pool, and I sat on one of the cushioned chairs next to a pretty Latina girl.

"First time taking a cruise?" the girl said, squinting over the top of her horn-rimmed sunglasses at me. "You look a little queasy."

"First time on a cruise like *this*," I chuckled, darting my eyes over her voluptuous figure, reminding me more of Salma Hayek than Jennifer Lopez. "I'm just not used to some of the...er, *distractions* on board."

"It's a bit of a shock at first," she nodded, glancing at my figure before I had a chance to notice that I too was completely naked from head to toe. "But you get used to it pretty quickly. Everybody's in the same boat, in a manner of speaking."

"Yeah," I laughed, peering around the pool at the scampering naked people. "With not too many places to hide."

"Why would you even want to?" the girl said, propping up her back rest to glance at all the eye candy. "You've got a beautiful figure, and there's so much to appreciate here. It's like being a kid in a candy store."

"Thank you," I said, peering at her dark medallions and erect nipples on her plump, round tits. "I was going to say the same thing about you."

"Lucia," she said, extending her hand into the short gap between our adjacent chairs.

"Jade," I said, feeling the oil in her slippery hands.

"Would you like me to put some sunscreen on your body?" Lucia said. "You look pretty pale for someone who's about to lie out in the sun for the first time."

"Um, sure," I said, lowering my chair to a flat position and lying facedown on the padded cushion.

Lucia stood up from her chair and squirted a couple of streams of lotion onto her palms then she kneeled on the sides of my lounge chair, straddling my ass. I could feel her warm pussy resting on my buttocks, and my clit tingled in excitement at the feel of her curvy body touching my naked figure.

"So where do you hail from?" Lucia said, spreading the lotion over my shoulders while I tried unsuccessfully to control my ragged breathing.

"Chicago," I said. "How about you?"

"My family's originally from Cuba. But I live in Miami now."

"Nice," I nodded. "But why are you taking a *cruise* when you already have all the sun you could ever want in Florida?"

"There's a few opportunities onboard this ship that you don't find in places like South Beach," she smiled, sliding her hands slowly down the center of my back while I unconsciously tilted my ass up higher.

"You mean like cavorting in the pool and dancing in the water fountain?" I said, glancing at a group of naked women skipping through a spray pad, squirting jets of water up toward their naked asses.

"Among other things," she smiled.

"So I'm beginning to see," I moaned as she rolled her palms over my cheeks and slid her fingers between the crack in my thighs.

I parted my legs a few inches further apart, inviting her to go lower, and she pressed her hands deeper into my cleft, sliding her fingers over my dripping labia. I grunted when I felt them touching my burning nub, and I tilted my ass even higher, giving her a clear view of my separated folds.

"Mmm," Lucia hummed, staring at my round ass and dripping slit. "That's a view I haven't seen this close-up for a while."

"Take your time and enjoy it for as long as you like," I sighed. "I'm enjoying your massage while I take in a few *other* arousing sights."

Lucia turned her head to see where I was looking, then she grinned while she kneaded her fingers deeper into the crease between my legs.

"Do you like watching women rub their bodies together?" she said, noticing me fixated on two women grinding their hips together while a stream from the splash pad jetted up between their legs.

"Sometimes," I shuddered, feeling her slip her fingers into my dripping slit. "I consider myself pretty versatile. I can go with the flow wherever I find myself."

"That's good to know," Lucia said, shifting back a few inches and pressing her right hand deeper into my slit while she massaged my hardening clit with the tips of her fingers and slipped her thumb into my pussy. "Because I think you'll find there's more variety onboard this cruise than you could possibly imagine."

"Unghh," I groaned, humping my hips against her hand while she slid the fingers of her other hand slowly through the crack of my ass. "I'm enjoying *this* particular variation just fine, thank you very much."

Lucia paused for a moment while she squeezed my cheeks and circled my pucker with her other thumb.

"Has anyone ever told you that you have a magnificent ass?" she said.

"Not lately," I grunted. "But whatever you're doing, don't stop."

"Fuck, no," Lucia said, pressing her thumb harder against my sphincter until it slipped inside. "If I had a *cock*, I'd be fucking those sweet cheeks right about now."

"Oh God," I hissed, feeling her fucking me from both sides with her two thumbs. "That feels incredible. I'm going to come soon if you keep doing that."

"Yes, baby," Lucia mewed. "Come for me. Come all over my hands while I watch your pretty ass shaking."

"Oh fuck," I growled, feeling my insides clamping down on her fingers while my pelvic floor muscles began contracting in a powerful orgasm. "Fuck, fuck, *fuckkkk*..."

Suddenly, Lucia's eyes began blinking while I squirted a series of jets over her lower hand and up the length of her arm toward her tits and face.

"Holy *shit*," she gasped, thrusting her thumbs further inside my holes while I gushed all over her arms and hands. "I'm not sure you needed this lotion after all. You're going to have a thick enough layer of lubrication on your backside to last you most of the afternoon."

"That's good to hear," I panted as my orgasm began to subside. "Because I've got a few ideas for my *other* side. I was hoping you could spread the lotion over my body in a slightly *different* manner..."

6

———

"Oh?" Lucia said, pulling her thumbs out of my holes and raising her hips off my ass. "What did you have in mind?"

I twisted my head and peered up at her with a lopsided grin.

"I was wondering if you could spread the lotion on me this time with something other than your *hands*."

She glanced down at me for a moment, then her face lit up with a broad smile.

"I think that can be arranged," she nodded, lifting herself up off the lounge chair to allow me to flip over.

When I turned around, I noticed her rubbing some lotion over the front of her chest, and I playfully pulled the bottle out of her hand.

"Let me return the favor," I smiled, sitting up and crossing my legs while facing the rear end of the lounge chair.

She sat down in front of me with her legs crossed like mine, and I glanced at her hips, noticing no sign of a bikini line over her pelvis or bare mound.

"Something tells me you won't need this stuff, either," I said, feeling my pussy twitching while I stared at her wet labia. "At least not to protect you from the *sun*. You've already got a beautiful tan all over your body."

"Perhaps we can use it for something *else* then," she nodded, clasping my hands softly and directing them toward her large, buoyant breasts.

"Exactly what I was thinking," I nodded, placing my palms over the top of her chest and sliding them slowly over her round orbs. "Though I'm not sure there's going to be enough in this bottle to cover all of you–"

"Well then," she smiled, uncrossing her legs and moving up closer to me while she wrapped her ankles around the back of my ass. "I guess we'll just have to *share* what we've got left on our skin."

"I like that idea," I said, separating my feet and pressing my pussy up against hers while I curled my legs around her ass.

As we rubbed our slippery tits together, we tilted our heads forward, locking in a tight embrace while our tongues danced in each other's mouths. For a minute or two, we were content to rock our hips together while we felt our pussies sliding against one another, then when it became apparent that it would be difficult to gain sufficient traction to stimulate our clits, Lucia pushed me gently back down onto my lounge chair, laying her body flat on top of mine while she ground her mound against me. I angled my hips upward, and when our nubs touched, I gasped, pulling her face down hard against mine.

By now, most of the bystanders sitting around the pool were staring at us locked in a passionate embrace, but I hardly cared. If anything, it only added to the excitement of the moment, seeing all the other naked passengers watching us making love in full view of the entire crew. I spread my legs further apart, and Lucia slid one of her knees between my thighs, interlacing our dripping labia, and I peered into her eyes, grunting loudly.

"Yes, Lucia," I moaned. "Fuck me with your pussy. Fuck me hard. This time I want to come all over your pretty *twat*."

"You're so dirty," she said, lifting her head and peering at me in mock indignation. "I like that. Let me see if I can get more comfortable..."

She raised up onto her knees, then she grabbed my right leg and tilted it over to the side until we were joined in a scissor position. I could feel her cunt pressing up against my slippery lips, and I rocked my head back, sighing in delirious pleasure. Out of the corner of my eye, I noticed most of the women and virtually all of the men with their hands between their legs, stimulating themselves while they watched the two of us tribbing on the shaking lounge chair.

"Fuck, yes," I groaned, pulling her knee further up my stomach while I rocked my hips hard against her pussy. "This is a much better way to spread our juices around. I'm going to come soon–"

"Wait for me," Lucia grunted, lifting my opposite leg and placing it between her swinging tits. "I'm almost there too."

But as soon I saw her lips gaping open with her pretty face nestled against my upturned leg while she clasped me tightly, I couldn't hold it any longer.

"Lucia," I panted. "I'm so sorry. You're so hot–"

"Gahhh!" she suddenly grunted, digging her fingernails into the flesh of my calf muscle while she convulsed between my legs and I gushed all over her ass.

We held each other tightly while we enjoyed a long climax, until the grunts of the surrounding spectators snapped me out of my trance. One by one, each of the passengers sitting on the lounge chairs around the pool began to gasp and shake while they tensed their arms over their quivering crotches.

"It looks like we started a bit of a chain reaction," I grinned, peering up at Lucia's flushed face.

"It appears that way," she nodded, glancing over toward the side of the deck where we watched a woman's ass humping another woman leaning over the railing. "And I think we should try to keep it going."

I glanced between the woman's legs and noticed a large ballsack slapping against her partner's cheeks, suddenly realizing it was a pretty transgender girl fucking her with her boy-cock.

"Yeah," I smiled as another dribble squirted out of my dripping pussy. "Maybe it's time to spread a *different* kind of cream over our bodies."

7

———

"Why don't we rinse off on the *splash pad?*" Lucia said after the two girls on the railing separated. "Maybe we can persuade some of the others to join us."

"Good idea," I said, feeling my body coated with a slippery mixture of sunscreen and love juices.

We scampered over to the spray fountain and swiped our hands over our naked bodies while the jets sprayed up toward our hips and breasts, and before long, the entire pad was filled with frolicking passengers. Lucia and I joined our bodies together over one particularly powerful spray, then we moaned in each other's mouths while the jet gushed over our merged pussies.

"You seem to be getting pretty comfortable prancing around in the nude aboard the ship," she smiled as we blinked our eyes from the spray splashing over our faces.

"Like you said earlier," I nodded. "We're all in the same boat. I don't see anybody *else* being shy about flaunting their wares."

We glanced at the pretty transgender girl sauntering

over in our direction, and I bulged my eyes when I saw her still half-erect tool. It must have been at least eight inches long even in its semi-tumescent state, but if you didn't glance below her belly button, you'd never know she wasn't anything but a full-blooded, gorgeous female. Her hips and ass were curved like a woman's, and she had a narrow waist accentuating her hourglass figure. But her best feature was her amazing tits. Tall and pointed and shaped like large cones, they seemed to defy gravity while the water jets bounced over them, sprinkling all over her pretty face. She noticed the two of us staring at her, then she walked over to our spot on the pad, pressing her cock against our slippery hips while she felt the water jet pulsing against her balls.

"Mmm," she hummed, batting her long eyelashes while she gazed at the two of us grinding our pussies together. "It's *delicious*, isn't it?"

"Are you referring to the *spray* or the view?" I said, glancing down at her big phallus, slowly thickening and rising upward.

"Both," she said, swinging her hips gently from side to side while her big organ slapped against the sides of our asses.

"It's getting even better *now*," Lucia said, reaching down to grasp the girl's hard-on and squeezing it between our two bellies.

"That was quite a show you put on earlier," the trans girl grunted while she humped her swelling glans against our stomachs. "You seem to have gotten everybody into a party mood."

"We noticed," I smiled, rolling my tits against hers while Lucia and I sandwiched her hard-on between our bellies. "We enjoyed *your* show almost as much as our own."

"Oh?" the girl said, darting her eyes between our two faces. "Do you like watching ladyboys fucking a girl?"

"Not as much as watching one fuck *two* of them," Lucia grinned.

"I'm not entirely sure how that would work," the t-girl said, obviously enjoying the attention Lucia and I were giving her. "I've only got one dick and you've got two holes."

"Fortunately, we've got some *other* sources of stimulation on this pad," Lucia said, twisting her body harder toward mine to trap the girl's big cock between our undulating hips. "Why don't you come all over our stomachs while we get our jollies standing over the water jets?"

"Works for me," the girl nodded, peering down at her swelling crown pistoning between our greasy bellies.

"Shit, that's hot," I groaned, watching our three sets of tits mashing together while her throbbing pole jackhammered between our bodies.

I didn't care if her breasts were fake. To me, they were the most magnificent tits I'd ever laid eyes on, and the combination of sensations watching and feeling the two women writhing their bodies against me while I felt the pulsing water spraying directly over my tingling clit was like nothing I'd ever felt before. Suddenly aware of how long I'd been immersed in my newest fantasy, I glanced at the timer in the lower right-hand corner of my helmet visor and noticed I only had five minutes left before my time ran out.

"Do you mind if I help you with that?" I said to the t-girl, sliding my hands down over the top of her bobbing pole, eager to watch her cream over Lucia's and my stomach before my session ended.

"You'll get no complaints on my side," the tranny huffed when I closed my fingers around her slippery crown.

"Nor *mine*," Lucia smiled, lowering her hands between

our rocking stomachs to grasp the t-girl's balls with one hand and the lower half of her shaft with her other hand.

I placed my left hand atop Lucia's with my right hand still massaging her bulb, and the ladyboy grunted loudly, thrusting her cock upward between our joined hands while the water spray showered our asses and pussies from below.

"Fuck yes," the ladyboy hissed as her cock head began to swell in my fist. "I'm going to spray my cum all over your pretty tits."

"Yes," I groaned, feeling my own orgasm beginning to well up inside me as I ground my pubis against Lucia.

"Oh my *God*," Lucia squealed, rocking her hips harder against our bodies while she squeezed the ladyboy's cock until it turned purple. "This is insane!"

"Huh, huh, huh, huh..." the trans girl huffed in an escalating crescendo of gasps until she jerked one final powerful thrust into our stacked hands, squirting long ropes of cum all over our shaking breasts. When I saw the ladyboy coming, I started squirting along with her, even though it was impossible to tell from all the liquid gushing and spraying over our joined bodies.

When the three of us realized we were climaxing together, we wrapped our arms around each other's shoulders and pressed our heads together, taking in the magnificent sight of our slippery bodies shaking and rocking together in a beautiful symphony of erotic pleasure. I hardly even noticed when my VR visor faded to black, closing my eyes and panting softly into my helmet, smiling with a huge grin at another exhilarating fantasy episode. I had no idea what kind of setting I'd choose for my next fantasy adventure, but something told me that this club was about to become my go-to place for sexual fulfillment.

I was able to book another two-hour session at the VR club three days later, but that didn't stop me from pleasuring myself whenever I thought about my erotic encounter with Lucia and the hot ladyboy. Whenever I took a shower, I'd rub my belly and my pussy at the same time, reenacting the experience of being sandwiched between the two pretty women. And when I woke up, horny after another hot dream, I'd flip over onto my stomach, imagining Lucia's pussy riding my ass while I humped my hands to one climax after another.

After reviewing the club's online menu again, I narrowed down my next scene preferences to either an upscale spa or a western dude ranch. When I noticed Jillian sitting at her desk on the day of my scheduled session, I decided to pop my head in to ask for her recommendation regarding the two options.

"Hi Jade!" she said, peering up at me with a big smile when I tapped on her door. "How did you like your last session? Was the nude cruise everything you hoped it would be?"

"I'll say," I nodded. "And then some. I enjoyed three distinct episodes within the individual scene, if you know what I mean."

"I think I do," she chuckled. "Glad to hear it's working the way you intended. What are you thinking of trying today?"

"I was hoping you could help me with that," I said. "Which do you think would provide more opportunities for something new? I've been vacillating between the Hammam Spa and the Western Dude Ranch."

"It depends what you're looking for," Jillian nodded. "The Hamman Spa is definitely refreshing and stimulating, but most of the performers are women, albeit hot and sexy Moroccan women. The Dude Ranch, on the other hand, has a lot of sexy cowboys to play with and offers some spectacular horse rides through the Rocky Mountains."

"Hmm, that's a tough one," I said, rubbing my chin. "Hot cowboys or hot masseuses. I'll have to think about that for a bit."

"Don't think *too* long," she grinned. "You won't want to lose any precious seconds immersing yourself into the fantasy once the timer starts. That is, if you want to enjoy as many *episodes* as you did last time."

"Don't worry," I laughed. "I won't waste any time once I'm strapped in. Between the probes embedded in the chair and the sensors in the bodysuit, it's pretty much a done deal."

"Let me know how it goes," Jillian said, then I thanked her for her help and I headed down to my scheduled room, closing the door softly behind me.

After I climbed into my suit and pressed the start button on the console, I scrolled through the menu quickly, finally settling on the dude ranch scenario. For the gender and sexual preference of my main character interaction, I chose male/bisexual, hoping I might have a chance to mix it up with more than one sexy cowboy at the same time. This time, I chose a thirty-year-old, white Caucasian with blond hair, hoping to channel a young Robert Redford from the movie Butch Cassidy and the Sundance Kid.

When the scene opened, I found myself leaning on the wooden railing of a horse paddock, watching a young cowboy trying to tame a wild stallion in the ring. The horse kept rearing up on his hind legs and kicking his front hooves in the air while the cowboy pulled on a long lead rope, keeping a safe distance away. After a few minutes, the horse began to settle down, and the cowboy moved in to pat his mane, then he grabbed his neck and pulled himself up onto the horse's back in one swift movement. The horse protested briefly, but when the cowboy pulled back on the reins attached to its mouth, the horse nodded its head, then began a slow cantor around the ring.

"That was pretty impressive," I said, peering up at the handsome cowboy when the horse circled around to my side of the ring.

"All in a day's work," he nodded, tipping his hat toward me. "You look new around here. First time visiting our ranch?"

"Yes," I said, glancing at stallion's rippling flanks. "First time this close to a *horse*, for that matter."

"Do you feel like giving it a try?" the cowboy said, pulling back on the reins and hopping off the horse as easily as a bicycle.

"On *that* monster?" I said, flaring my eyes. "No thanks. I'll wait for one of your tamer and smaller ones. I'm liable to break my neck if I get on that thing."

"Suit yourself," the cowboy said, unlatching the gate to the paddock and leading the stallion toward a nearby barn.

"I'm sure we can get you fixed up with something more to your liking when you're ready for your first excursion."

"I'll look forward to that," I said. "Where do I go to sign up?"

"You'll find the reception area in the main lodge," the cowboy said, pointing toward a large post-and-beam house nearby.

"Thank you," I nodded, holding out my hand to the cowboy. "My name's Jade, by the way."

"Holt," he said, gripping my hand with a scruffy leather glove.

"Pleased to meet you," I smiled. "I'll look forward to seeing what *else* you can tame during my stay on the ranch."

"It'll be my pleasure, ma'am," he nodded, clicking his tongue and pulling on his horse's lead to steer him in the direction of the barn.

I watched him walking away while staring at his tight ass in his loose-fitting jeans framed by the leather chaps resting over his hips, then I suddenly felt myself panting as I leaned on the paddock railing for support.

"Now *that's* a real man," I sighed, feeling my pussy throbbing while I imagined him riding me as confidently as he had the wild stallion.

I peered around the ranch, noticing the landscape stretching out for miles in every direction, with soft grasslands toward the northeast, and tall, white-capped mountains facing the southwest. The whole thing looked like something out of an old Western, and I soaked up the spectacular view, inhaling the scent of burning firewood drifting from the chimney of the lodge, then I headed toward the front door, planning to book my itinerary. Then I remembered what Jillian had said about being careful not to waste a precious second of my session, and I glanced back in the direction of the barn, listening to the sound of horses softly braying in their stalls.

"Fuck it," sighed, turning back toward the barn. "I'm the one in control of what happens to me in these fantasy games. Let's see if I can persuade Holt to teach me a few *other* tricks of his trade."

But when I entered the open barn door, there was no sign of him, nor the big stallion he'd tamed in the paddock. I walked slowly down the straw-covered aisle between the stalls, noticing the animals peering out at me casually while gnawing softly on piles of hay. I saw the big stallion from the paddock resting in one of the stalls near the end of the aisle, then I heard a different kind of panting and grunting sound coming from behind the gate of the adjacent wash station. But when I peered around the corner, my eyes flew open when I caught Holt and another cowboy locked in a passionate embrace with their jeans down by their ankles while they rubbed their cocks together through the opening in their leather chaps.

Holt looked up when he detected movement at the side of the stall, and I turned away with a flushed face.

"I'm sorry," I stammered. "I didn't know you were...I mean, you know...*busy*."

"Was there something you needed?" he said, pulling up his pants while his partner turned away to hide his erect cock.

"No," I said, glancing down at his swelling crown poking out of the top of his jeans. "Or at least, I didn't think so until now."

Holt paused for a moment while he glanced at his partner, then he nodded slowly as a wide grin stretched over his stubble-lined jaw.

"Would you like to *join* us?" he said.

"If I'm not interrupting anything," I nodded, suddenly feeling the panties of my jeans sticking to my dripping pussy.

"The more the merrier," he said, dropping his jeans back down to the floor while his thick organ bobbed over his tight balls.

His partner turned back around to face him, and they slapped their cocks together playfully while they caressed each other's muscular, furry chests.

"This is Boone," Holt said, sliding his hands down over his partner's hips and clenching his fingers over his tight ass.

"That's quite a sight," I said, hastily unclasping the buttons on my flannel shirt while tearing some of the eyelets, and throwing my bra over the top of the wash bay door. "I haven't seen two cocks this pretty in quite some time."

"Happy to oblige," Holt smiled, twisting his hips in unison with Boone while I kneeled down in front of them on the damp concrete pad of the wash station.

I grasped their two cocks with each of my hands and closed my eyes while I felt the heat of their shafts rubbing against my cheeks as I nuzzled my nose into their furry bushes. These were no metrosexual boys from the big city with their neatly trimmed and landscaped crotches. These were real *cowboys,* wearing only what God gifted them, knee-deep in the middle of God's country. I twisted my head and licked up the sides of each of their shafts in turn, then I slowly stood up, grabbing their sacs in my palms and squeezing them gently.

"I don't suppose you'd be willing to share those pokers with a little *lady* for a change of pace?" I grinned, kissing them on the undersides of their neck and smelling their musky cowboy scent.

"I suppose that depends on what you had in mind," Holt said, sliding his hands over the tops of my breasts and circling my nipples with his middle digits. "Because there's two of us and only one of you."

"This isn't my first rodeo," I chuckled, reflecting back on the t-girl's similar comment from my nude cruise session. "You guys seem to like rubbing your cocks together. Let's see if I can give you a little extra *lubrication* and a tighter sleeve to work with."

Holt cocked his head and glanced at Boone's widening eyes, then he peered back at me with a raised eyebrow.

"You mean...*DP?*" he said, shaking his head.

"Yes, but not in the way you might be imagining it," I smiled. "Instead of taking you separately in each of my holes, I want to see if I can fit both of you inside my *pussy* at the same time."

"*God*, yes," Boone panted when he saw me taking off my jeans and panties, noticing my shaved and glistening snatch.

"We're going to have to do this carefully," I said, glancing at each of them, one at a time. "Lie down on the floor facing away from each other, with your balls nestled up against one another. I'll take care of the rest."

"Okay..." Holt said, still not entirely sure what I had in mind.

They lay down on the cold, wet floor with their bobbing cocks betraying their rising excitement, then I straddled their hips, slowly squatting over their upturned poles. Even though I chose to face Holt with my front side, something told me Boone wouldn't feel too left out viewing my backside while I bobbed over their throbbing tools. When I felt their tips swiping against my cheeks, I reached down between my thighs and pulled their erections together, pointing their burning crowns toward my dripping slit. It took a few seconds to ease both of them inside me, but once they parted my slit, it was pretty easy to lower myself over their throbbing erections until they were all the way inside my pussy.

"What do you think?" I said, glancing at Holt, who looked like he'd died and gone to heaven. "Is this as good as jerking off into each other's *hands*?"

"Holy shit," he huffed. "This is *sooo* much better."

"How about *you*, Boone?" I said, twisting my head halfway around. "How are you doing back there?"

"I'm enjoying the view," he grunted, flexing his buttocks while he tried to move his cock inside my hole.

"It's not the same kind of ass you might be used to," I nodded, rolling my hips softly over their joined cocks. "You're probably not used to fucking a *girl* from behind."

"It's pretty sweet either way," he shuddered. "And I've still got a fine view of Holt's cock and balls from this position."

"Good," I said, humping their hard-ons faster while I gripped Holt's flexing pec muscles for support. "Because I want you to watch *both* of your cocks pulsing while I gush all over your balls."

"No way," Boone hissed, suddenly clamping his hands over the sides of my ass.

"Way," I nodded, feeling myself getting ready to burst in more ways than one. "Let me feel you both come in my pussy. This is the most fun I've had playing ride-em-cowboy in a long time."

"Nnngh," Holt groaned, spreading his mouth wider apart while he reached up and squeezed my tits progressively harder. "Oh *fuckkk...*"

As his upper body began jerking on the floor in front of me, I noticed Boone's boots slapping together while he grunted in simultaneous climax behind me. When I realized they were both coming inside me, I clenched my teeth, feeling my climax wash over me, then I groaned loudly as I gushed my juices hard over their connected balls, hollering like a drunk cowgirl.

Now I see why they call it a dude ranch, I smiled to myself while I felt their cocks throbbing inside my dripping pussy. These guys are the real deal. I wonder what *other* surprises await me on this little western adventure...

9

fter the three of us separated and got ourselves cleaned up, I went back up to the lodge to check on the other excursions available at the guest ranch. The woman behind the desk handed me a brochure, and we discussed the various activities ranging from trail rides to whitewater rafting to fly fishing. When she explained that the trail ride would include an overnight campout, my mind was already racing ahead at the idea of finding a new playmate to bed down with.

I booked the tour but when she told me it didn't start for another three hours, I peered at the timer in the lower corner of my visor to see how much time I had left. With only one and a half hours left in my scheduled session, the last thing I wanted to do was sit around waiting for the next scene to get started. I decided to call up the VR support agent to see if I could fast-forward ahead.

"VR Help," I announced into my helmet.

"Yes, Jade," the soothing robotic voice of the online assistant replied. "How can I help you?"

"Am I able to advance my scene to a particular point of my choosing?"

"Yes," the agent said. " I see that you've scheduled a trail ride as part of your dude ranch session. Where would you like me to advance to?"

I paused for a moment, remembering how Jillian had said the horse trip through the Rocky Mountains offered spectacular views, then I nodded my head, giving the virtual agent my next instruction.

"Can you put me atop one of the easier horses and place me in the tour group halfway up the mountain?"

"Of course," the agent said. "Please stand by."

A moment later, the scene inside my visor changed from the crackling fireplace of the lodge to a column of horses walking up a wooded trail beside a raging river, while my chair rocked slowly from side-to-side, simulating the feeling of riding atop a large mare. I glanced down at the steep embankment leading to the valley below, and I felt my heart pounding in my chest, unsure how to steady myself on the shaking horse. I glanced ahead of me, watching another guest bobbing softly atop her mount, then I peered behind me, noticing Holt taking up the rear of the line.

"Are you sure it's safe to be walking on this skinny trail so far above the valley below?" I said to him.

"We've taken this track hundreds of times without an accident," he nodded. "Your horse has strong legs and excellent balance, so there's nothing to worry about."

"It's not the *horse* I'm worried about," I said, struggling to keep myself centered in the saddle while my mare rocked from side-to-side.

"You're working too hard to fight the animal," he said while he studied my movement. "Try to relax your muscles and go with the flow. Let the *horse* do the work while you synchronize your movement with her. You'll be less sore afterwards and you can enjoy the view more."

I paused for a moment while I peered at the rider ahead of me, noticing her swinging her hips gently atop her saddle while her horse ambled up the path. Her butt was firm and round while clad in tight jeans, and suddenly I was conscious of a different part of my body tensing while I watched her. I loosened my grip on the horse's reins and relaxed my leg muscles, mimicking her erect posture in the saddle, beginning to feel my body rocking in tandem with my horse.

"That's the idea," Holt nodded, focusing on the movement of my hips in the saddle. "The idea is to *sway* with the horse rather than clench your thighs over it."

"Sounds familiar," I grinned, reflecting back on our previous encounter in barn's wash stall. "But I see what you mean about enjoying the view."

"It's pretty amazing, isn't it?" he said, peering up at the snow-capped peaks soaring thousands of feet above us.

"Beautiful," I nodded, panning over the enormous mountain range extending hundreds of miles into the distance. "Almost as beautiful as the view from inside the barn earlier today."

"Different strokes for different folks," he chuckled.

I soaked up the pretty view of the thin tendrils of waterfalls streaming down the steep hillsides while listening to the sound of the gurgling river below us, then I peered at the column of horses curling around the trailhead, wondering when we'd set in for the night.

"When will we reach our campsite?" I said to Holt, turning my head back in his direction.

"Not for another couple of hours, after the sun drifts over the top of the mountains."

I glanced at my helmet timer and noticed it flipping past the one hour marker, then I called up the online assistant again.

"VR Help," I said.

"Yes, Jade," the robotic voice replied.

"Can you fast forward me to the campsite before we turn in for the night?" I said, hoping to catch a glimpse of the *other* side of the pretty girl riding ahead of me.

"Of course," the assistant said. "One moment..."

Suddenly the scene changed to show a group of people sitting around a campfire in a clearing overlooking a turquoise-colored lake nestled between a ring of mountains, and I glanced at the girl sitting on the log next to me, recognizing her checkered shirt and long, curly hair. The shadow of the flames from the fire danced over her pretty face, and I peered down at her plump cleavage straining against the buttons of her shirt while she held a long stick toward the fire, roasting a marshmallow over the edge of the flame.

"Oh my God," I sighed, watching the reflection of the moonlight over the tranquil lake. "Have I been transported to *heaven*, or am I just imagining this?"

"Maybe a little bit of both," she chuckled, turning her head and smiling at me. "It's pretty hard to imagine a place closer to heaven than this idyllic place nestled in the mountains."

"You seem like an old hand at this," I nodded, watching her draw her stick away from the fire while blowing softly on her smoking treat. "At least judging by how confidently you were riding your horse."

"This is my third time visiting the ranch," she nodded. "The scenery out here is spectacular, and the staff are super-helpful."

"Yes," I smiled, glancing toward the other side of our

circle at Holt and Boone chatting with some of the other guests. "So I'm beginning to learn."

"Would you like a marshmallow?" she said, pulling her lightly charred confection off the end of her stick and raising it toward my lips.

"Um, sure," I said, surprised at how hot it was when she popped it into my mouth. "Mmmft," I huffed, opening my mouth to ease the discomfort of the searing cream.

While I awkwardly chewed on the spongy candy in my mouth, some of it dribbled down the side of my chin, and the girl raised her right hand, swiping it gently off my face.

"Thanks," I chuckled. "It's been a while since I've had one of these."

"No worries," she said. "There's a bit of an art to getting the texture just right on both the inside and the outside. My name's Kelly, by the way."

"Jade," I said, clasping her hand gently. "Since you've done this before, I was wondering if you could tell me where we turn in for the night. Or do we sleep under the stars like the cowboys in the movies?"

"Never fear," Kelly said. "Every other horse carries a two-person tent. We're expected to pair up by gender to save space and provisions. You're welcome to overnight with me if you'd like."

"Thank you," I smiled, placing my hand on her knee and squeezing her thigh gently. "Do we have anything other than marshmallows to eat? I could almost eat a *horse* after that long trail ride. Not literally, of course."

"I think Boone and Holt are planning to cook up some hamburgers on the portable grill," Kelly nodded, motioning toward the two cowboys preparing the food next to the fire.

"Excellent," I smiled. "I could do with some more *meat* right about now."

~

K elly and I chatted around the fire for the next hour or so while we finished our dinner, then we set up our tent under a pine tree overlooking the lake. It was quite small, just barely big enough for the two of us to lie down side-by-side, and I peered at the vinyl floor covering, feeling the lumpy ground beneath us.

"Do we have anything more comfortable to lie on?" I said, wrinkling my forehead.

"I packed a yoga mat along with the sleeping bags," she nodded. "We might both be able to squeeze on top of it if we share one bedroll."

"I'm game if you are," I smiled, suddenly feeling my pussy twitching at the idea of nestling our bodies together in the tight confines of a shared sleeping bag.

"Sounds like a plan," Kelly said. "I just need to go pee before turning in for the night. I'm hearing the call of the wild."

"Me too," I said, grabbing a flashlight. "Is there a designated spot where we can do our business?"

"Unfortunately not. We'll have to do it like the bears and the wolves. Squatting in the bush along with the rest of the woodland creatures."

"Bears and wolves?" I said, flaring my eyes open in fright. "Maybe I don't have to go after all."

"Come on, silly," Kelly said, grabbing my hand and pulling me out of the tent. "The fire will keep the animals at bay as long as we don't stray too far from the campsite."

The two of us scampered to the other side of a nearby tree and lowered our pants while squatting over a log, then we giggled listening to the sound of our sprinkles on the soft ground. Suddenly, we heard the sound of a low growl somewhere in the brush behind us, and we pulled up our jeans, running back toward our tent and zipping up the front cover. We laughed while clasping our arms around one another, staring into each other's eyes with wide pupils.

"Are you sure we're safe in here?" I said, tapping the flimsy canvas covering of the tent.

"That's what our *tour guides* are for," Kelly nodded. "I've seen them at the shooting range, and they're pretty handy with their pistols."

"Yeah," I said, glancing through the mosquito-net window of our tent at the next tent over where I saw the outline of two figures hunched over one another in their shared tent, illuminated from the backlight of the fire. "Except they seem pretty distracted with firing something *else* right now."

Kelly scooted up next to me and peered out the small window at the two men fucking each other bare-back, then her eyes widened.

"Holy crap!" she said. "I had no idea they were gay!"

"Well, they're not *completely* gay, as I discovered earlier today. It's not only their pistols they're pretty handy with."

"Really?" Kelly said, turning her head toward me and bulging her eyes. "You had a *three-way* with them?"

"More of a one-on-*two*-way. But yeah, it was pretty hot."

"You've got to tell me all about it," Kelly said, clutching my hands excitedly. "I've always fantasized about being with two men at the same time."

"Let's talk about it under the covers," I nodded, pulling off my clothes and throwing them to the side of the sleeping bag. "It might be easier to explain if I can *demonstrate* it while lying next to you."

"Fuck, yes," Kelly said, ripping off her clothes and

throwing them atop mine, then jumping into the sleeping bag and zipping it up around our naked bodies.

"Mmm," I purred, feeling her smooth skin and round breasts pressing up against mine. "This is quite a bit softer than what I experienced on the hard floor of the barn."

"How did you guys do it exactly?" she said, slipping her thigh slowly between my legs. "Did they fuck you one at a time, or did you service them together?"

"Let me show you," I said, flipping on top of her and grinding my wet pussy against her mound. "I positioned them with their cocks facing each other, then I humped them, cowgirl-style on top."

"Fuck, that's hot," Kelly groaned, digging her fingernails into my back while I ground my pussy against hers.

"You have no idea," I grunted, spreading her legs wider apart while I tilted my pussy between her legs. "But I'm kind of enjoying feeling something softer and wetter between my legs tonight. And besides, you're a better kisser..."

"Mmm," Kelly moaned into my mouth as we rolled our tongues together, rocking our hips in rising pleasure. "This is *another* fantasy I've always dreamed about. You feel incredible."

"I know what you mean," I shuddered, feeling the climax to another VR episode rapidly coming to an end. "This has been one crazy fantasy adventure after another..."

10

The next day, I returned to the Virtual Reality Club and reviewed the online menu, looking for my next erotic fantasy. After the exciting dude ranch experience, I wanted another outdoor adventure, and I paused when I saw the listing for a nudist colony. The idea of being immersed in a setting where everyone was walking around completely naked, where I could openly stare at their bodies and choose my next sexual partner without any restrictions, appealed to my libertine side.

I climbed into the full-body suit and leaned back in the animatronic chair and pressed the start button on the console. For the gender and sexual preference of my main character interaction, I chose a ladyboy/bisexual, hoping I might have a chance to mix it up with a variety of different genders and body types. Mindful of the stereotype of nudist camps colonized by fat, old couples, I scanned the profiles for trans girls and selected one who looked like a young Marilyn Monroe. With full, pointy breasts, an hourglass figure, and a glowing face with big pouty lips, she looked like a dead-ringer for the famous movie star. Everything except the big swinging dick hanging down between her long, slender legs.

God, I love this place, I sighed to myself, feeling my clit twitching against the tight latex fabric pressing against my dampening pussy.

The scene opened with a group of naked men and women playing a game of volleyball on a sandy pitch, and suddenly a ball arched over the top of the net, angling directly toward my face. I threw up my arms defensively, and the sensors on the suit slapped my hands when the faux orb hit my palms, bouncing back over the net in the direction of a pretty blond girl. I only had a couple of seconds to notice the unusual appendage hanging between her legs before the ball bounced back in my direction, and this time I leapt up before it reached me, striking it back hard toward her legs. The ladyboy crossed her arms protectively over her crotch, and the ball bounced sideways into the sand.

"Woo-hoo!" one of my teammates yelled, and I glanced over at a young stud with a tight swimmer's build, giving him a high-five.

I hardly had time to scan the bodies of the other buff players on both sides of the pitch before the ball lobbed back over the net in my direction, with the pretty ladyboy serving from her side of the court. I grinned when I saw that she seemed to be targeting me, and I flexed the fingers of my hands, sending the ball softly back in the air, where the stud with the swimmer's build redirected it toward another guy waiting at the front of the net. When the ball arched directly over his head, he leaped up into the air and slammed the ball back down into the sand before anyone on the other side could reach it.

"Nice," the swimmer's build said while each of us moved

one position clockwise on our side of the court to alternate the role of server.

As he lobbed the ball back over the net toward the other side, I quickly scanned the tight asses of the players standing in front of me, and the toned figures of the players on the other side. Unlike the caricature of nudist camps filled with sedentary, old people, this one seemed to be populated with hot, buff, active singles who had no reservations about strutting their wares for everyone to see. And it was quite the spectacle, with everyone's muscles and body parts flexing and swinging while they bobbed, jumped, and weaved to keep the flying ball in the air.

While my robotic chair twisted and rolled to mimic my movements across the sandy court, it didn't take long for me to build up a healthy sweat in my latex suit. I was glad when the match finally ended, with our side walking away with a decisive victory. Soon after, everybody walked over to the edge of a tranquil lake set in the middle of a forest reserve and dove into the crystal-clear water to cool off, stepping out of the water to lie down on the grass to dry off in the overhead sun.

"Nice match," the pretty trans girl said, striding out of the water and walking up toward my position on the grass, looking for all the world like Ursula Andress emerging from the surf in the infamous Dr. No scene while James Bond stared at her, trying to keep his composure.

"Thanks," I nodded as she lay down on a beach towel and sat next to me, dripping from head to toe. "I had a little help from my teammates."

"If I didn't know any better," she smiled, "I'd think you were targeting me directly with your overhead slams."

"Well, you *do* make a tempting target," I grinned. "With so many sensitive body parts to protect..."

"Touché," she said, holding out her wet hand over her beach towel. "My name's Willow. You're new around here."

"Jade,' I said, clasping her hand and feeling my pussy twitch while I tried not to stare at her thick tool glistening between her thighs.

"So what's your story?" the trans girl said, running her eyes shamelessly over my naked figure. "Why did you come to the camp? For the fresh air, to shake off your inhibitions, or for some other reason?"

"All of the above," I smiled, glancing down at her crotch and noticing her semi-tumescent pole resting against the side of her wet thigh.

"Well, welcome," Willow said, spreading her knees further apart to give me full viewing access to her magnificent tool. "Let me know if you have any questions or need me to show you around."

"I was wondering where we put in for the night," I nodded. "And where the mess hall is. I'm famished after that invigorating game–"

"I've got an extra bunk in my room," Willow smiled. "You're welcome to stay with me if you've got nowhere else to go."

"That would be lovely, thanks," I nodded while a drop of lubrication dribbled down the inside of my thigh.

"Where's all your stuff?" Willow said, darting her eyes curiously around my empty embankment.

"Um, I'm not sure," I laughed, realizing the game settings offered limited functionality in setting up the sexy scenes.

"No worries," she said, standing up and holding out her hand to help me off the grass. "Let's get you set up, then we'll head over to the cantina to get you something to eat."

As she led me in the direction of one of the tents, I stared at her exquisite ass, flexing and bouncing tantalizingly while she rocked her hips, striding confidently past the side-glancing stares of the other camp denizens. When we reached her tent, I noticed two bunks positioned one over the other, with a small table and locker on the other side of the small enclosure.

"I'm on the *bottom*," Willow said, pointing to her well-made bunk. "Do you mind being on top?"

"Er...no," I stammered, glancing down at her thick phallus, pointing a good eight inches below her shaved mound, even seemingly flaccid.

"Are you hungry?" Willow said, noticing my gaze drifting down below her ripped abdomen.

"No...yes...I mean, not for *food*. Suddenly I feel hungry for something *else*–"

"Mmm, I know what you mean," Willow said, glancing at my hardening nipples. "I've had my eye on you ever since we started that last game."

"I'm glad the feeling's mutual," I smiled, taking one step closer toward her and caressing the tops of her upturned tits with one hand.

"It's more than *mutual*," Willow said, placing her hand between my legs and sliding her fingers over my dripping slit. "I think half the guys on your team wanted to pound something other than the volleyball once you joined the group."

"Not as many as those who wanted a piece of that pretty *dick*," I grinned, grasping her pole with my free hand and squeezing it tightly. "At least, judging by how many people were staring at you while we walked back toward our tent."

"They'll just have to *imagine* what it's like to fuck either one of us for the time being," Willow smiled, grabbing my hand and pulling me toward her cot. "Still feel like being on top?"

"Yes, please," I panted, staring at her rising erection, now standing almost ten inches in front of her belly.

"Good," she said, lying on her bed and spreading her legs far apart, inviting me to sit on her bobbing pole. "Because I want to look at you while you fuck me."

"My pleasure," I said, crawling onto the bed and positioning my hips over her hard-on while I slowly lowered myself over her throbbing python.

"Mmhhh," Willow groaned as I took her inside me.

"God, you're big," I rasped, feeling her thick tool spreading me apart.

"*Too* big?" she said with a wrinkled brow. "Am I hurting you? Do you want to switch positions–"

"No way," I said, pushing her back down onto her bunk. "This is perfect. I want to play with those beautiful tits while I fuck you. You're just the right size."

"Yes, baby," Willow said, rocking her hips slowly against mine. "Let me feel your pretty ass on my balls. You're a magnificent specimen..."

"Not as pretty as *you*," I grunted, sliding my pussy back and forth over her gyrating hips, feeling my clit beginning to tingle from the friction against her hard pubis.

"Shit, I'm going to come soon," Willow hissed, digging her fingernails into the side of my hips while I fucked her harder.

"Fuck yes," I groaned, feeling the pressure building up inside my stomach. "Spurt your spunk inside me. You are so fucking hot–"

Suddenly, she raised her hips off the surface of her mattress, bumping my head against the bottom of the overhead bunk, and I leaned down, kissing her on her lips while we groaned in each other's mouths and rubbed our tits together. When I felt her cock pulsing inside me, I grunted loudly and gushed my juices all over her balls, and her eyes flared open in surprise while she grabbed my buttock cheeks, pulling my pussy harder against her. But about halfway into our synchronized orgasms, we heard some muffled voices outside our tent and we peered up toward the small, uncovered mesh window over the bed, noticing two teenage boys staring at our joined bodies with wide eyes.

"*Shoo*, you two!" Willow huffed, rising up and pulling down the privacy flap while shaking her head at me.

"Sorry about that," she said, peering at me with a flushed face. "Sometimes it's hard to find any privacy around here."

"No worries," I chuckled. "It is a nudist camp, after all. I imagine privacy is the *last* thing on the minds of most of these people..."

11

After we recovered from our orgasms, Willow and I left our tent, looking for the young peeping Toms who'd invaded our privacy. After a few minutes of searching, we noticed them slipping behind the back of a barn near the edge of the woods, and we decided to follow them to see what other kind of trouble they were getting into. We ducked into the brush and crept slowly through the forest until we saw them crouching behind some water drums, kneeling next to one another.

"Look," Willow whispered when we reached the edge of the clearing. "They're touching each other's cocks!"

"Should we give them shit for spying on us?" I said.

"Let's just watch them for a while," Willow smiled, staring at their hard-ons. "I think this might be their first time–"

"Having *sex*, or playing with each other?"

"Both. They're pretty new around here and they've been sporting woodies from day one. Most of the other guys have grown pretty accustomed to all the nudity."

"They hardly look *legal*," I said, glancing at their soft

asses flexing while they humped their hips into each other's hands. "Should we even be watching them?"

"The camp has a policy about everyone being at least eighteen years of age to walk around in the nude, so don't worry," Willow nodded.

"They look kind of uncomfortable about touching one another," I said. "Maybe we should go over there and offer them a helping hand..."

"Give them a few more minutes," Willow smiled. "It's not like they haven't touched their own cocks before. I'm sure they'll figure out how to stimulate one another if we give them enough time."

I watched the two youngsters groaning while they humped each other's hands, then one of them crouched a little lower, taking his partner's erection into his mouth while he bobbed his head softly up and down over the other boy's organ.

"I see what you mean," I nodded, drifting my hand between my legs while I watched the two youths exploring one another.

"It's pretty hot watching them having gay sex for the first time," Willow said, reaching out to stroke her own hardening tool while she stared at the teenagers along with me. "It reminds me of my *own* fledgling youth..."

I glanced at Willow's pretty figure while she stroked her cock with two hands, wondering what her experience had been growing up as a transgender girl.

"When did you have your first same-sex experience?" I said. "I mean, with another *man*–"

"I was pretty young," she nodded. "Before my sex-change operation. It was in high-school, behind one of the portables during recess. We were both kind of curious..."

"Is that what made you *convert*? Were you always attracted to boys?"

"Sexual preference is a different mindset to gender orientation," she said. "I always liked dressing up like girls and playing with dolls. It wasn't until later that I realized I liked having sex with both men and women."

"Do you feel like going down there and showing them how it's done? They probably haven't had sex with *girls* before either–"

"Or ladyboys," Willow chuckled. "We'd probably raise their interest in more ways than one. But I'm having almost as much fun just watching them."

"Yeah, this is crazy-hot," I nodded. "There's nothing like watching two young people discover their sexuality for the first time."

Suddenly, the boy getting the blowjob buckled his knees and clenched his ass, leaning forward while he grasped his friend's head and emptied his seed into his partner's mouth. The second boy raised his head and spit into the grass beside the water barrels, twisting his face into a disgusted expression.

"Or watching their *reaction*," Willow laughed. "I'm pretty sure that first boy isn't gay, judging by his reaction."

"I'm not so sure about his *friend* though," I smiled, watching the boy who'd emptied his load hungrily gobbling down his friend's hard-on while he bent down on all-fours to service him.

"Yeah," Willow nodded, staring at the second boy expertly sucking the other one's erection while he rubbed one hand on the shaft and squeezed his friend's balls. "Something tells me that's not the first time he's sucked another boy's cock."

"Speaking of," I said, noticing the head of Willow's dick

emitting a drop of precum as she began to stroke her pole faster. "Would you like something a little softer and wetter, stroking that beautiful instrument?"

"If you're referring to your *lips*," Willow nodded, lifting her hands from her dripping dick and thrusting it forward between my breasts. "I'd love to fuck your pretty face. There's something about watching another person worshipping your cock that I particularly enjoy."

"I see what you mean," I chuckled, noticing the boy on the receiving end of the blowjob staring at his partner sucking his dick while he dug his fingernails into his hair.

"Mmm," Willow hummed while I encircled her glans and flicked my tongue around her corona. "I see this isn't *your* first time sucking a cock either..."

"Or sucking a *ladyboy*," I smiled, squeezing her balls with one hand as I reached up to pinch her hardening nipples.

"Fuck, that feels good," Willow grunted, grabbing my head and pulling me harder down over her swelling erection.

"Playing with your *nipples* or squeezing your *balls*?" I murmured, lifting my head temporarily off her organ.

"Both. You sure know how to please a girl..."

"And a *boy*," I smiled, lowering my head back down over her throbbing cock and pumping my mouth over her shaft while I squeezed her shaft with two hands.

"Just like the other teenager behind the shed," Willow grunted, darting her eyes between my head bobbing up and down on her organ and the two youths rocking their bodies together in oblivious bliss.

"How would you like a cock *sandwich* the next time around?" I smiled, watching the two boys grunting out of the corner of my eyes while I glanced up at Willow's rapidly flushing cheeks. "I'm pretty sure these two boys will have plenty of juice left in the tank for a pretty ladyboy when they're finished."

"Yeah," she hissed, gaping her mouth open as she neared orgasm. "But I have a *different* kind of dish in mind when we join them in a few minutes. I'm going to show them how to mix pickles and avocados in an entirely novel kind of way..."

I smiled when I heard the youths squealing as the second boy came in his friend's mouth and Willow followed suit soon after. I savored the taste of her honey while her organ pulsed in my mouth, swallowing it all down and gripping her shaft tightly until she'd spent her entire load. When she finally finished shaking, she pulled her dripping organ out of my mouth, glancing down at me approvingly.

"Fuck, that was hot," she panted, caressing the sides of my cheeks as I raised up to kiss her.

"Watching me go *down* on you, or watching the two boys sucking each other?" I grinned.

"Both," she nodded.

I saw some movement out of the corner of my eye and watched the two boys lie down in the grass while they played with their still-hard tools as they caressed each other's ass cheeks.

"Are you ready to mix it up a bit?" I smiled.

"We can't leave any of that to waste," Willow nodded, glancing at the two boys' erections. "Like my momma used to say, it's a crime to leave any food on the plate..."

12

———

Willow and I approached the back of the barn slowly so as not to alarm the two boys, and when they saw us, they instinctively covered up their erections.

"Is that any way to greet new guests?" Willow smiled, swinging her hips from side to side to slap her half-erect dong against the side of her thighs. "You're not the *only* ones with excited willies out here."

"Were you watching us?" the first boy said, worried that their secret had been exposed.

"No more than you were with *us* a little earlier," she nodded. "You really shouldn't go around spying on people in the privacy of their own homes."

"Sorry," the second boy said. "It's just that we've never seen a lady with a *penis* before..."

"Do you *like* it?" Willow smiled, swinging her dick from side to side. "You seem to have an affinity for other people's cocks."

"It's very beautiful," the first boy nodded.

"And *large*," the second boy grinned.

"Do you want to *touch* it?" she said, stepping closer to the boys while swinging her tool tantalizingly close to their faces.

"Can we?" the second boy said, reaching his arms out slowly.

"Perhaps we should introduce ourselves first," Willow said, twisting her hips just out of their reach. "My name's Willow, and this is my friend Jade."

"I'm Richard," the first boy said. "And this is my friend, William."

"Well, *Dick and Willie*," Willow smiled. "I see you've already gotten a head start playing with each other's stiffies. Are you interested in learning what it feels like to be with a *woman* for a change?"

"Fuck, yes," Richard nodded. "We're both virgins that way–"

"But only *half*-virgins when it comes to *ladyboys*," Willow chuckled. "You already seem to know your way around a *dick* pretty well by now."

"Not one connected to someone as pretty as you," William grinned.

"Oh, that's so sweet," Willow said, turning to wink at me. "If I didn't know any better, I'd think these two were trying to pick us up."

"Well, they *are* very handsome," I smiled, glancing at their bobbing erections. "And they seem to have come fully prepared for the occasion."

"Mmm," Willow nodded. "But we have a bit of a conundrum. We've got three cocks, but only one pussy. How could we possibly all stimulate one another at the same time?"

"True," I said with a sly grin. "But there's one thing these boys still haven't tried yet. What if we *stacked* ourselves, one on top of the other?"

"You mean, via the *back door*?" Willow grinned, staring at the boy's cute butts.

"We could actually alternate, front-to-back," I said. "You could be on the bottom, then Willie here could sit on you, and I could in turn sit on his dick, leaving Richard with free access to all of us."

The two boys peered at one another with a confused expression, but their bobbing cocks betrayed their under-lying interest in my proposal.

"But I don't have a *pussy*," William said, shaking his head.

"Well, not a *girl* pussy," Willow grinned. "But a tight pocket all the same..."

"I don't know," William said, staring at Willow's giant erection. "Do you think you could fit that thing inside me?"

"There's only one way to find out," Willow said, sitting down on the grass next to him and spreading her legs far apart. "Something tells me you *like* boys. This is just another way for you to explore their bodies."

William stared at her upturned pole, then glanced at his friend, as if seeking his approval.

"Don't look at me, man," Richard smiled. "This whole thing was your idea in the first place. You're the one who's *gay*, not me."

"Okay," William said, noticing a dollop of cum spilling out the tip of Willow's bobbing cock. "Which way do you want me to sit on it?"

"Facing me, of course," Willow smiled. "That way, I can see the look on your face while I'm fucking you."

"And you can watch her pretty tits," Richard nodded.

I watched Richard's eyes widen as his friend kneeled

over Willow's erection and he slowly lowered himself down over her hips.

"How'd you like to play with *both* of our breasts?" I said to him. "We can put Willie's hard-on to good use while I sit on his dick, then you can stand in front of me while you fuck my tits."

"Holy shit!" Richard nodded excitedly. "That sounds hot!"

"And I can play with his balls from the other side," Willow grunted as William flexed his anus around her phallus.

"I can squeeze them together from behind her back to create more friction," William groaned, bobbing his hips up and down over Willow's girl-cock while his eyes rolled back in his head in delirious ecstasy.

"Looks like you boys have got it all figured out," Willow smiled, grabbing the sides of William's ass and squeezing his cheeks while she fucked him up the ass. "Let's get this party started."

When I saw William's erection flapping up and down while he bobbed his hips over Willow's pole, I kneeled down in front of him facing her, then I angled my hips backwards until I felt his tool enter my hole.

"Oh God," he groaned when he felt my wet pussy envelop his organ. "This is insane! You have got to try this after me, Ricky. This is way better than just sucking each other off."

"Maybe," Richard said, placing his feet on either side of Willow's chest and pointing his dick toward my bouncing breasts while he stared at our naked bodies. "But there's something else I'd like to try first..."

I reached out and pulled his dick toward my tits and placed it upright against my cleavage, then I pressed my breasts together to form a pocket for him to stimulate himself. As he began to rock his hips upward to create more friction, I tilted my head down and encircled his bobbing head between my lips, giving him a blowjob unlike anything he'd ever experienced before.

"Holy fuck, Willie!" he panted, watching me sucking his dick while he pistoned his organ between my boobs. "Did you ever imagine we'd be with these two hot chicks when we snuck up behind their tent?"

"*Fuck*, no," William panted as Willow rammed her dick deep inside his cavity. "I feel like I've died and gone to heaven. I never *dreamed* sex could be this wild and crazy."

"We're just getting started, boys," Willow smiled, raising her upper body onto her arms and sticking her face between Ricky's flexing cheeks, tickling his anus with the tip of her tongue.

"Oh fuck, I'm going to come!" he suddenly growled, clenching his buttocks together while he thrust his cock hard against my chest, erupting buckets of come all over my face and tits while I squeezed his balls.

Soon after, his friend William squealed in pleasure as I clamped down over his dick and squirted my juices all over Willow's stomach and his tightening balls.

"Eeeii!" he screamed, emptying his seed deep inside my pussy while my contractions pulsed against the base of his cock.

When Willow saw that the rest of us were climaxing together, she dug her fingernails into the sides of William's hips, shuddering as she climaxed inside his clenching ass while the four of us groaned in delirious union. After we all came down from our powerful orgasms, we separated from one another and tumbled onto the grass next to each other, panting and smiling with satisfied grins.

"*Still* think you're not interested in anal sex?" Willow

grinned, turning to glance at Richard, who was staring up at the daylight sky with stars in his eyes.

"If it feels anything like having my butt licked while I'm fucking a girl's tits, I'm game for *anything*," he sighed, flinging his arms to the side of his chest in utter exhaustion.

13

After my exciting VR adventure at the nudist colony, I took a couple of days' rest to recover and plan my next escapade. There was something about the nudist camp that I'd found fresh and exciting. Being able to see all the participants in the buff and choose my sexual companions appealed to my free-spirited side, but after scanning the club's online menu, I couldn't find any similar programs. I decided to check in on the club's hostess during my next visit and see if she could offer any suggestions. After booking another two-hour session, I saw Jillian sitting at her desk the next day, and I knocked on her open door, distracting her temporarily from her desktop monitor.

"Hi Jade," she said, recognizing me from my previous visits. "How did you like your last session? I noticed that you booked the nudist camp scenario."

"It was pretty hot," I nodded. "In fact, I was looking for something similar, but I couldn't find anything on your online menu."

"What kind of scene were you looking for, exactly?" she said.

"Something where everyone is already in the nude," I said. "It speeds up the process of getting into the action, if you know what I mean."

"I think I do," Jillian chuckled, turning her monitor around in my direction and tapping her fingers on the keyboard. "You've already done the nude cruise, and now the nudist camp. Let's see what else might arouse your interest..."

She stopped scrolling when an image of two naked, dripping women appeared on the screen, then she peered up at me.

"What about this one, the *Steam Room*? The setting is something like a Russian bath, except in this case, the scene is populated with your choice of men or women–"

"Or *both*?" I grinned.

"Of course," she laughed. "Whatever strikes your fancy. That's the beauty of our simulated experience. You can choose the profile of the characters you wish to interact with, and you can always change it around if the program isn't working for you."

"Can I choose *two* main characters this time?" I said, feeling my panties dampening while I stared at the two voluptuous women in the picture.

"Absolutely," Jillian nodded. "Every program allows you to specify up to five unique characters per scene."

"That's probably a few more than I can handle," I said, remembering how difficult it was to get four of us together in the last episode. "But this one looks right up my alley. Thanks for the suggestion, I'll let you know how it goes."

"Please do," she smiled. "We always like feedback from

our customers so we can constantly improve our programs and design new ones to meet their needs."

I can think of one special way you can meet my needs, I smiled to myself when I exited her office and walked down the corridor in the direction of my designated cubicle. *At some point, I need to figure out how to get into her pants for real. These simulated scenarios are exciting, but there's no substitute for the real thing. That girl is seriously hot.*

When I got into my room and locked the door behind me, I climbed into my suit and pressed the start button on the console, scrolling through the menu until I found the Steam Room program. After seeing the two girls on the profile screen, I chose female/lesbian for the two main characters, one Caucasian and one African American, both in their early twenties. I felt a bit greedy always choosing characters to interact with who were considerably younger than my mid-thirties, but that was one of the attractions of the virtual reality club. I could choose whoever I wanted to have sex with, without any guilt or repercussions.

When the scene opened, my visor suddenly became clouded, and I found myself walking down a steamy corridor with doors on both sides. Some of them were closed and some were open, and as I walked past the open doors, I slowed my pace to glance at the naked people sitting on the padded benches inside. Some were single males sporting woodies, and some were lone females posing in equally provocative positions. I paused for a moment when I saw two men frotting their cocks together while they sat cross-legged facing one another, kissing each other as they moaned in each other's mouths. It reminded me of the two youths from my last episode, where Willow and I introduced them to some new techniques.

But it wasn't until I reached an open door with two

women caressing one another inside that I stopped dead in my tracks. Just as I had requested in my profile selection, they were both young and nubile, with slender, sylph-like figures and full breasts covered in water droplets from the warm steam jetting out of the room's side vents. I glanced at their bare pussies revealed by their splayed legs as they knelt toward one another with one knee angled upward. The contrast between the one girl's pale, white skin and the African-American's girl's chocolate-brown skin was stark, only adding to the eroticism of the scene.

"Have you got room for one more?" I said, staring at their glistening vulvas, separated by only a few inches.

They ran their eyes up and down my naked body, then they nodded approvingly, motioning for me to enter the room.

"Close the door behind you," the white girl said, curling her index finger in a come-hither motion. "We don't want any men crashing our party."

"Works for me," I nodded, turning around and latching the door closed while I tilted my ass upwards to give them a view of my own dripping pussy.

As I walked toward them, sitting together on the padded stainless steel bench, a warm mist permeated my VR helmet, and I felt myself beginning to sweat slightly. I loved the way the designers of my suit had thought of everything to recreate the setting I'd chosen, and I felt the fabric around my vulva beginning to tighten as I began to lubricate my lower regions with a different type of fluid.

"You're beautiful," I said to the two girls, stroking the sides of their moist torsos while I ogled their model-perfect figures.

"You're pretty hot yourself," the African-American girl said, reaching out to tweak my hardening nipples with her right hand.

"How would you like to do this, exactly?" I grunted, feeling the sensors inside my suit pinching my nipples with the attached probes.

"You're the one who came to *us*," the white girl said, drawing the tip of one finger sexily up the middle of my stomach. "We've already had our turn with one another. What did you have in mind?"

I peered at their bodies for a moment, reflecting back on the way Willow and I had sandwiched ourselves between the two boys in the nudist colony episode.

"Could I lie *between* the two of you?" I said.

"Sure," the pretty African-American girl said. "Which of us do you want on the bottom, and which one on top?"

I glanced at the two women, then I smiled when I saw the black girl's pink labia flare open as a dribble of lubrication rolled down the inside of her thighs.

"Can you lie face-up while I rub my body against you and the other girl lies on top, rubbing my backside with her naked body?"

"That'll work," the African-American girl nodded, flipping over to lie on the padded bench, slowly spreading her legs apart.

I knelt overtop of her then slowly lowered my body over hers, pressing my breasts against her wet tits while I ground my pubis against her dripping vulva.

"Unghh," she groaned when she felt our clits touching.

"That's a pretty *ass* you've got," the white girl said as she crawled on top of my back, grinding her pussy against my buttocks.

The mixture of sweat and water vapor from the steam-infused room made the sliding of our bodies against one another effortless, and before long, all three of us were grinding our bodies together, groaning into each other's mouths and ears while we sandwiched ourselves in a three-way pile of writhing flesh. Our skin colors seemed to blend perfectly together, from the ebony-colored skin of the black girl on the bottom to my own caramel-tan color to the pale, alabaster skin tone of the girl on top. I turned my head and darted my eyes from one to the other, trying to take it all in, but when the girl on top slid three fingers into my pussy from the backside of my ass while I fucked the black girl's pussy with my mound, I felt my pleasure growing expo-nentially.

"Mmmm," I groaned, pressing my hips backward to thrust her fingers deeper inside my twitching pussy. "Fuck me with your fingers. I'm going to come soon on your friend's pretty pussy."

"Yes," the white girl panted, humping my flexing buttocks harder as she rolled her tits over my slippery back. "And I'm going to come all over your sweet ass–"

When she turned her hand sideways, slipping her thumb into the black girl's pussy while simultaneously ramming her fingers into my dripping snatch, that was enough to put all of us over the edge of our teetering orgasms.

"Guhhh!" the black girl hissed as she jerked her hips hard against mine and I gushed all over her shaking legs.

Seconds later, the girl on top followed suit, squirting between our joined legs while she quivered atop our convulsing figures, gripping the sides of my back while she lowered her head next to the black girl's and mine, squealing in tandem with the two of us while we enjoyed the most exotic threesome of our lives.

14

———————

After we all recovered from our orgasms and flopped into each other's arms, I realized we'd never even gotten each other's names. We'd been too busy fucking each other and in too much of a rush to begin rubbing our bodies together to talk much. As hot as it had been having spontaneous, anonymous sex, I wasn't ready to leave yet, and I thought we should get to know each other a little better if we were going to continue our little tryst.

"Do you girls know one another?" I said, peering at their flushed faces.

"You mean other than in the *biblical* sense?" the white girl said.

"Yes," I chuckled. "That's one way to get to know each other."

"We're *partners*," the black girl said. "We live together. We just come here to spice up our sex life and keep it fresh."

"And to find compatible partners," the white girl nodded. "We figured it would be better to participate in *consensual* cheating rather than swinging on the down-low."

"Makes sense," I nodded. "This setup allows you to vet your partners before jumping into bed together and offers a modicum of privacy."

"Plus, it's remarkably clean for a sex club," the other girl said. "The stainless steel beds and vinyl cushions are cleaned after every person leaves the chamber, and the hot steam helps to sanitize everything."

"They're going to need to do an *extra* thorough cleaning after that last episode," I chuckled, sliding my finger across the dripping bench pad, coated with our combined juices.

"You squirt just like me," the white girl nodded. "Jasmine's been trying to figure out how to do it for ages, and she's a little envious of my ability."

"It's not as hard as it looks," I said. "I actually attended a women's workshop where they trained us how to do it."

"Can you teach *me*?" Jasmine said, suddenly propping herself up on one arm. "It's so hot when Lily comes all over me."

"Sure," I said. "But now that I know both of your names, perhaps you should know mine. I'm Jade..."

"That's a beautiful name," Jasmine said.

"As are yours," I smiled, tracing a line down their stomachs toward their glistening slits.

"What do you want me to do?" Jasmine said as her stomach quivered in anticipation. "I mean, in order to *train* me–"

I paused for a moment as I contemplated the best way to gain access to their pussies while monitoring their technique.

"Why don't the two of you lie down on the bench, facing one another, with your legs apart? That way, I can show you how to stimulate yourself and massage your G-spots to express your ejaculation."

"I like the sound of that," Jasmine said. "But where will *you* be so we can stimulate you at the same time?"

"I'll kneel over you in the sixty-nine position this time," I said. "That way, I can watch both of you more closely and monitor your progress. But you should probably concentrate on your *own* pleasure at first. I'll have just as much fun watching you squirt as I would getting off with you."

"Okay," Jasmine said. "But we'll be happy to return the favor once we're finished. I've been wanting to suck your pussy pretty much from the moment you appeared in our doorway."

"Save that thought," I smiled. "But first, let's get you squared away."

The two girls twisted around until their pussies were facing one another, then I instructed them to lift their knees into an elevated position, with their feet resting beside each other's hips.

"Okay," I said, peering at their black and white vulvas. "This will work better if you start out stimulating *yourselves* at first. I want each of you to insert your middle and index fingers partway into your slits, up to the first knuckle..."

The two girls did as I instructed, and they moaned softly, lifting their heads to peer at one another.

"Now, curl your fingers upward toward the front side of your vaginas. You should feel a round bump about the size of a marble."

"I can feel it," Jasmine panted. "Is that my G-spot?"

"It is," I nodded. "But more importantly, it's also the location of a special gland that every woman has, called the Skene's Gland. It's analogous to a man's prostate gland, insofar as it emits a special fluid when you orgasm that aids in the fertility process."

"Why do some women emit more fluid than others?" Lily

said. "I always thought I was *peeing* when I gush during climax."

"Not at all," I laughed. "You can actually see and smell the difference if you collect some of your ejaculate in a glass the next time you come. The Skene's fluid is colorless and odorless, whereas urine usually has a yellow tinge and a slight ammonia odor."

"Good to know," Jasmine chuckled. "Now, how do I make this thing work? I want to come all over Lily's pussy just like mine when we climax together."

"You need to massage the bump where your G-spot is located steadily and softly, almost like you're playing with your clit. This will stimulate the area and bring more fluid into the gland, causing it to swell. When you climax, it will eject the fluid, especially if you exert enough pressure."

"How long does it normally take?" Jasmine said, growing a little frustrated with her inability to climax.

"You've got to be patient," I nodded while watching the two girls fingering each other inches apart. "Try to relax and enjoy the sensation of stimulating yourselves internally. Did you know the clitoris is actually ten times larger than what you see on the outside, and actually surrounds the entire inside of your vagina?"

"I had no idea," Lily said, beginning to rock her hips gently as a soft flush began to roll over her chest.

"You can raise your heads and look at one another if that helps," I said, feeling my own pussy beginning to drip from excitement watching the two girls rocking their hips together.

"I'd rather stare at *your* pretty pussy," Jasmine said, beginning to grunt more loudly as her fingers started to move more rapidly inside her pussy. "I'm dreaming of sucking you and feeling you gush over my face–"

"It doesn't take much to get me going," I chuckled, feeling the familiar pangs of a budding orgasm building up inside me, just from watching the sexy girls jilling themselves.

"It feels like I need to pee," Jasmine said, suddenly scrunching up her face.

"That's a *good* sign," I said, panting along with the other girls. "That means you're getting close. It's a normal sensation when you're close to ejaculating. But don't worry, it's the *Skene's* gland preparing to empty, not your bladder."

"Oh fuck, I'm going to come," Jasmine grunted. "Are you sure I can let it go? It feels like I'm going to pee–"

"You won't," I groaned along with her, feeling myself approaching the tipping point. "Let it go. I assure you, the feeling will be like nothing else..."

Suddenly, Jasmine raised her hips off the padded mattress and curled her fingers inside her quivering pussy, then she squealed like a little girl as she started jetting her fluids against Lily's snatch while her friend grunted in tandem with her.

"Oh fuck, Jasmine," Lily gasped while she gushed her juices out of her pussy between her two fingers. "I can feel you coming on my pussy! God, this is so hot. I'm coming with you, baby!"

The sight of the two women climaxing and squirting all over their exposed pussies at the same time was too much for me, and without even touching myself the entire time, the excitement of the scene was so overwhelming that I came soon after the other two women, gushing a waterfall over Jasmine's contorted face while we all shook our bodies together. It took almost a full minute for each of us to finish squirting and convulsing, and when our orgasms finally began to abate, I dropped down next to the two friends, staring at their wet bodies and the pool of liquid rippling in a puddle on their still-quivering stomachs.

"Well?" I said, peering at Jasmine's flushed face. "Was it as good as you imagined? Are you happy you know how to squirt now?"

"Oh my God," she huffed. "It was even better than I expected. There's something about the feeling of really letting go when you come that makes it incredible. I had no idea I had this in me, *literally*."

"I'm glad you liked it," I smiled. "Next time, we'll have to show you how to ejaculate in other ways. You won't always want to use your *fingers* when you're stimulating your partner."

"You came without even *touching* yourself," she nodded. "Can you teach me how to do that too?"

"One thing at a time, girl," I chuckled. "Whatever happened to your eating my pussy?"

"I'd rather *drink* it," Jasmine smiled, rolling over and sticking her face between my legs.

15

In my inverted position, I was already close to Lily's pussy, and when she saw Jasmine going down on me, she angled her hips toward my face, creating a perfect triangle formation, with each of our head's buried in the other's crotch. Normally, I wasn't into the sixty-nine position since it didn't allow me to focus on my own pleasure as much, but in this *three-way* configuration, I had an open view of the other girls' squirming bodies and their faces sucking each other's pussies.

"Mmmft," Jasmine groaned when she felt Lily's tongue dancing over her dripping slit.

"Nnngh," Lily huffed, rocking her pussy into my face.

"Hufft," I joined in the symphony, licking up Lily's sweet juice while she sucked Jasmine's flaring bud.

"Holy shit," Jasmine said, briefly coming up for air between my legs. "This is three times as good as doing it *solo*!"

"Like I said," Lily nodded. "Adding new partners every now and then keeps it fresh and exciting."

"No kidding," I hissed, grinding my pussy into Jasmine's puffy lips. "This is a first for *me*, too."

"Why don't we see if we can all come at the same time?" Jasmine grunted. "It will be wild watching us all squirting between each other's legs."

"Do you think you can do it without internal stimulation?" I said.

"Well, I'm feeling like I need to *pee* again, so I'm guessing that's a good sign–"

"Just don't pee on my *face*," Lily huffed. "I'm not into golden showers."

"I dunno," I chuckled. "It might be fun. That could be a first for all of us, too."

"I'm gonna be spurting *something* pretty soon," Lily grunted. "Watching Jazz sucking your cunt is driving me crazy, and I can feel the pressure building up inside..."

"I'm getting close, too," I nodded. "What about you, Jasmine? Are you almost there?"

"If you'll stop talking for a moment and continue sucking on my clit, it won't take long..."

"Okay," I said, sticking my face back between her partner's legs. "Just give us some non-verbal clues, so we can try to coordinate our orgasms with you–"

"Oh, I'll give you non-verbal clues, alright," Jasmine smiled, sucking my nub hard into her mouth and biting the end of it with her teeth.

"Guhhh," I hissed, feeling the rising pressure inside my hips approaching the bursting point.

"Uhnnn," Lily panted next to me, rocking her hips harder against my face when I stuck my tongue inside her dripping hole.

"Fuckkkk," Jasmine squealed, tightening her thighs around Lily's head.

Suddenly, she let out a deep growl as her hips began jerking against Lily's face, and her friend blinked her eyes when Jasmine started spraying her juices all over her face. When I saw Jasmine climaxing, I opened my floodgates, gushing a tidal wave over her gagging mouth, and when Lily saw our combined juices flying between our bodies, she howled in unison, squirting her own juices into my eager mouth while I swallowed it all down. It was the most incredible sight, watching the three of us with our faces embedded in each other's pussies as our juices squirted and sprayed over our shaking tits and abdomens like a circular water fountain. I didn't want to let go of Lily's shaking hips, and after we finished coming, we just lay quietly on the oversize pad, savoring the taste and smell of our joined sexes.

"That was possibly the longest and hardest climax I've ever experienced!" Jasmine said when we finally relaxed our bodies and flopped over onto our sides.

"So you're finding that ejaculation adds to the experience?" I said, peering at her dripping vulva.

"Fuck, yes," Jasmine nodded. "I don't know how I can ever pay you back. You've improved my sex life immeasurably."

"I'm happy I could help," I smiled. "But believe me, it was just as much fun feeling you gush all over my face as it was to feel you sucking my pussy."

"That was pretty hot," Lily nodded. "But there's still one way we haven't tried stimulating each other. Can you imagine what it would feel like to squirt our juices together while we're grinding our *pussies* together?"

"You mean tribbing?" Jasmine said, glancing up at Lily. "But how could we do that three ways? One of us would have to be left out–"

"Not necessarily," I said, propping my arm up so I could

look at both of them. "I can think of at least one way we can connect our pussies together at the same time. It will require a bit of contortion to pull it off, but I learned this at another one of those women's workshops..."

"Holy shit, Lil," Jasmine said. "We have got to go to one of these workshops sometime."

"It certainly sounds like another way to meet new partners in a safe and consenting environment–"

"And you'd be surrounded by like-minded women, with no men to spoil the mood," I nodded.

"I'm sold," Lily said. "But first, show us this new technique for three-way tribbing."

"Okay," I grinned. "Which one of you is the most flexible? It's going to require a bit of gymnastics..."

"That would probably be Jasmine," Lily laughed. "She was an All-American in the balance beam at college."

"That's perfect," I said. "That means she'll be on the bottom again this time. I want you to lie on your back and raise your knees as far as you can toward your chest while spreading your legs apart."

"I guess we really *are* getting to know one another better," Jasmine chuckled, rolling over and prostrating herself in the indicated position while Lily and I stared at her gaping pussy.

"Okay," I said to Lily. "Now you're going to squat on top of her, tilting your body forward..."

"Like this?" Lily said, following my instructions and resting her hips on top of Jasmine's upturned ass.

"A little bit further forward," I said as I positioned myself behind their connected asses, facing away from their bodies. "The trick is to spread our legs wide enough and curl our bodies forward far enough to touch our pussies together."

I shimmied my ass backward a few inches until I felt my

buttocks rubbing up against theirs, then I angled my hips and pressed myself against their joined bodies until I felt their wet slits touching mine.

"Holy fuck!" Jasmine said. "This feels insane!"

"Three times as good as usual?" I chuckled.

"Well, at least *fifty* percent better," Jasmine said, smiling at Lily, whose face was resting next to hers.

"Okay," I said. "Now here's the hard part. We'll need to move our hips in synchronicity in order to stimulate our clits simultaneously. It might require a bit of shifting position while we're rubbing our bodies together..."

Jasmine and Lily started groaning as they began rocking their hips together, but their ass cheeks kept me from sliding my pussy far enough into their creases, and try as I might, I couldn't maintain enough friction on my vulva and clit to keep myself stimulated while they became increasing aroused.

"Try angling your hips a little more into a forty-five degree direction, Lily," I instructed, shifting the position of my knees so I was angled slightly in the opposing direction.

"How's *this*?" Lily said, twisting her hips partially to the side.

"Perfect," I moaned, feeling my slit slipping in between their cracks until I felt our slippery juices commingling while we rubbed our cheeks together.

"Oh God," Jasmine groaned when she felt our clits rolling over one another.

"Just when I thought it couldn't get any better," Lily nodded, humping her hips faster against our joined pussies.

"Just wait until we *come* together," I smiled, feeling another orgasm welling up inside me. "It's an otherworldly experience gushing our juices together over our connected cunnies."

"I can't hold back any longer," Jasmine suddenly huffed beneath us. "This feels way too good. Here it comes..."

When Jasmine started gushing her juices again against our joined asses and vulvas, it tripped both Lily and me over the edge, and for a few precious, heavenly seconds, we all quivered our asses together while we savored the sensation of our juices spraying over our gaping pussies as we shuddered and squealed in three-part harmony.

"Fuck me," Jasmine gushed when we all collapsed beside one another on the padded cushion. "You have got to hook us up with those special seminars you've been going to. Lord knows the new tricks we might learn when we connect with some other women."

"It'll be my pleasure," I smiled. "Though I'm already thinking of some new ways we can expand our repertoire of techniques just between the three of us..."

16

———————

fter the allotted time for my scheduled VR session abruptly ended, I went home exhausted but fully satisfied. My triple tryst with the two sexy girls in the steam room had exceeded my expectations, and I had a cramp in my lower abdomen for three straight days from climaxing so hard so many times. But after a week or so, I was itchy to get back into the suit and lose myself in another simulated fantasy.

I scrolled through the club's online menu for a new scenario, and when I saw a picture of three girls wearing clinging t-shirts with erect nipples darting through the wet fabric, I paused, feeling my pussy twitching in my pants. *Spring Break*, I thought, looking at the title of the episode. That sounds like a lot of fun. A bunch of horny young college students letting loose on the white sands of Florida? *Sign me up!*

I booked another two-hour session, and when I started up the session on my next trip into the studio, the scene started with me walking along the mile-long Pompano Beach of Fort Lauderdale, filled with boisterous, half-naked college kids splashing through the surf and playing games in the sand. When I saw a group of topless women playing volleyball against an equally buff and tanned group of young men, it reminded me of the sexy episode where I'd met the pretty transgender girl, Willow, at the nudist camp.

I paused for a moment to watch the action, feeling my pussy moistening in my scene-designed bikini, then I turned my head in the direction of a loud cheer coming from further up the beach. A woman's voice was blaring over a loudspeaker, and there was a large crowd gathered around an elevated platform with a group of sexy girls lined up in a row. Curious to see what all the commotion was about, I headed over to the grandstand and wedged my way toward the front of the crowd.

"I hope everyone enjoyed that last exhibition," a pretty girl wearing a yellow bikini said from the center of the stage, raising a microphone to her mouth. "But this next one is going to take the concept of a wet t-shirt contest to an entirely new level..."

A group of young studs surrounding the stage hollered in approval, then the MC smiled, motioning to the girls standing on either side of her. Each of them was wearing a tight-fitting, white t-shirt over a skimpy bikini bottom, and I soaked up their sexy bodies while my eyes darted over their braless torsos with their nipples softly darting the fabric. Some of them had full, plump breasts and some had obvious, surgically enhanced balloons, and some of them had small, firm tits that made my mouth water.

"Instead of spraying *water* on the contestants," the MC said. "This time we're going to spray a different type of fluid on their shirts. We're going to see which one of you sexy ladies can squirt the furthest the hardest to arouse their pretty buttons–"

"Woo-hooo!" the men hollered, high-fiving each other in excitement, hardly believing their luck being able to witness such a provocative display.

"I *thought* you guys might be up for this one," the MC smiled. "So now, we just need some volunteers. Which of you ladies is willing to step up onto the platform and put on a new kind of waterworks show?"

The boys hollered again, turning around to peer at the other women watching the proceedings, encouraging them to go up onto the stage. But nobody seemed willing to expose themselves this openly, so the MC reached into a wooden chest resting on the stage beside her and pulled out a couple of familiar-looking toys. I recognized the long, white handle of the Magic Wand vibrator, but each of the devices also had an extra appendage connected to the ball on the tip, looking like a stubby, curled finger.

"I thought some of you might be a bit reluctant to show your wares," the MC said. "So to make it more interesting, we're going to give each volunteer a special aid to get you into the mood. Some of you might recognize this device as a vibrator, but we've added a little attachment to stimulate your G-spots and get your juices flowing. If you've never tried one of these things before, I guarantee you'll find it's like nothing else you've ever experienced."

While the men hollered and pushed their girlfriends toward the front of the stage, most of the women seemed reluctant to step forward to reveal their lower parts. I stared at the sexy girls on the platform, feeling myself getting wetter by the moment, then I brazenly stuck up my hand, feeling brave and reckless.

What could go wrong? I thought to myself. *It's just a simulated program. Nobody will ever know that I've actually stripped down and jilled myself to orgasm using a giant vibrator while a bunch of horny college students cheered me on.*

"I'm game," I shouted over the raucous noise, smiling at one of the girls on the stage.

The cheering suddenly stopped, and the boys turned around to peer at me, wondering what a middle-aged housewife was doing crashing their college party. But their ogling eyes betrayed their prurient interest in me as they scanned my tight ass, yoga-toned abs, and firm breasts, barely concealed in my string bikini.

"Um, okay..." the MC said over the mic, scanning my figure while the crowd slowly separated away from me. "What's your name, ma'am?"

"Jade," I smiled. "And I'm not afraid to strut my stuff. Plus, I"m a prodigious squirter, with or without the aid of a vibrator. I'm willing to help if you need some extra volunteers."

The MC paused as she scanned the stunned faces of the other spectators surrounding the stage, then she raised the microphone back up to her mouth, nodding approvingly.

"What do you say, boys?" she grinned, darting her eyes over the eager faces of the young men who were nodding excitedly in anticipation. "Should we let this sexy momma join one of our games?"

"Wooooo!" the boys yelled enthusiastically, jumping up and down to signal their approval.

"Okay, Jade," the MC said, motioning for me to climb up the steps. "Come on up here and make yourself comfortable." She motioned to a row of wooden lounge chairs positioned a few feet in front of the girls wearing t-shirts. "Since you're our first volunteer, you get to choose the first position."

I glanced at the lineup of t-shirt-clad women and smiled

at the one nearest the end with a tight ballerina's figure and a cute, girl-next-door face. I pulled off my thong and shook my shaved crotch teasingly in front of the crowd, then I sat down on the angled lounge chair, spreading my knees apart for the girl in front to see my dripping pussy. A loud cheer rose from the crowd as the men signaled their readiness to get the festivities started, then one-by-one, other girls walked up onto the stage and took off their bikini bottoms, sitting beside me on the stage in front of the other girls who were staring at their naked snatches.

This should be good, I thought to myself as a rivulet of liquid dribbled out of my slit and down the inside of my thighs. The nipples of the girl opposite me quickly hardened, and I licked a circle around the edge of my lips, signaling how much I was looking forward to squirting my juices on her pretty figure while I rammed the big dildo inside me.

17

"Okay, ladies," the MC smiled after all the lounge chairs had been filled with half-naked co-eds spreading their legs apart. "Are you ready to get this party started?"

The boys in the crowd cheered wildly while the girls blushed softly, looking at one another with uncomfortable expressions, wondering what the hell they'd signed up for.

The MC handed each of us our own Magic Wand vibrator with the G-spot adapter, then she raised one up in her hand to show us how to use it.

"For those of you who aren't familiar with this little toy, allow me to demonstrate the controls," she said.

She tapped the first blue button below the tip, and the round head started shaking softly.

"This first button turns the device on, then the one below it sets the pulse pattern..."

She pressed the next button a few times, and the vibrator made a series of alternating pulse sounds.

"You've got four choices to choose from: *constant, wave,*

pulse, and cha-cha. You may wish to experiment with the different patterns until you find the one you like the most."

Then she tapped the last button a few times, and the device rumbled a little louder each time.

"This bottom button sets the *speed*, from low to medium to high to toe-curling-intense. But you better be careful about setting it too high too fast, because this thing really packs a punch. You might want to start with the lower settings to get yourself in the mood, then work up to the higher speeds when you feel yourself getting ready to squirt. Any questions?"

'How do we position the *curved* piece?" one of the girls in the chairs said, turning the wand around in her hands while she peered at it with a wrinkled forehead.

"It's meant to be inserted inside," the MC smiled. "If you turn it so the curved part faces *upward*, you'll find it's a perfect stimulant for your sensitive G-spot. It's specially designed to get your juices flowing and maximize your squirting ability."

I had to chuckle at the ingenuity of the contest designers. Not only had they dreamed up the sexiest possible demonstration to satisfy any voyeur's wildest dream, they'd also chosen the perfect instrument to stimulate our G-spots and help express the women's natural ejaculation ability. Although I assumed the women who had volunteered already possessed some kind of natural squirting affinity, the special Magic Wand adapter would take our spurting abilities to an entirely new level. While I glanced at the lineup of girls standing in front of our chairs, I wasn't sure if the volunteers would be able to reach them from the separated distance, but it hardly mattered. The simple act of watching them stimulating themselves with the oversize vibrator would be enough to satisfy any observer's craving, not least, the ones sitting in the chairs.

As the men and women standing around the stage cheered and hollered in encouragement, the girls lying in the chairs slowly tapped the buttons on their vibrators, inserting the curved attachments into their slits while they spread their legs further apart. It didn't take long for each of them to begin moaning and rocking their hips in growing excitement while the boy's cocks hardened in their tight Speedos and their girlfriends started caressing their tools, equally mesmerized by the spectacle on the stage.

For my own part, I was happy to take my time ramping up my pleasure, having previously experimented with the device, savoring the sight of the sexy boys and coeds staring at me and the rest of the girls while we pressed the vibrating instrument against our shaking vulvas with two hands. The pretty girl standing in front of me seemed particularly fascinated by my display, darting her eyes alternately from my flushed face to my bobbing breasts to my glistening vulva while I sent rivers of lubrication dripping down the insides of my thighs and over my tightening butt cheeks.

As the girls beside me began to groan more loudly and turn up the intensity settings of their vibrators while curling their bodies into a pre-orgasmic position, the MC noticed their rising pleasure and motioned for the girls wearing the t-shirts to step closer toward their partners.

"I think we've almost reached the magic moment," she smiled. "You girls standing opposite might want to move a little closer if you want to get your tops thoroughly drenched. Half the fun is seeing your pretty nipples fully exposed when the girls come all over your chests. You better get ready, because it's about to get pretty wild and crazy up here..."

The girls wearing the t-shirts slowly stepped forward, then most of them kneeled down in front of their partners, leaning their bodies forward to encourage them to spray their juices over their heaving chests. I wasn't sure who was enjoying the show more, the young men who were hooping and hollering at the side of the stage, or the girls with the bird's-eye view of their partners' dripping pussies preparing to jet their juices over their waiting bodies.

Moments later, the first masturbating girl began shaking her hips and wailing out loud as she spurted a series of jets onto her partner's shirt, soaking the area around her nipples and highlighting her hard nubs while the other girl gaped at her convulsing vulva. One-by-one, each of the other girls soon after erupted in likewise fashion, squealing and jerking their hips in delirious union while they held the shaking vibrator tightly against their quivering twats. Some of the women shot narrow, hard squirts in a series of pulses toward their opposing partners, some of them barely dribbled out of their slits, spraying small droplets on the bottom halves of their partners' shirts, and some of the women gushed a torrent out of their convulsing slits, soaking their partners completely.

Each of their eruptions ratcheted up my pleasure another notch, until, when it was finally my turn to climax, I raised my hips high off my chair and gushed a firehose directly into the face of my surprised partner. Blinking her eyelashes while trying to keep her focus on my twitching pussy, she shoved her hands under her bikini bottom, trilling her clit rapidly to climax soon after me. While we stared into each other's eyes, gaping our mouths open in shared pleasure, I barely heard the cheers and gasps of the surrounding crowd, who were equally mesmerized by our erotic performance.

Oh my God, I sighed, leaning forward to kiss the girl as we both came down from our intense orgasms. *Who dreams up this shit? Because I've got enough fantasies left in the bank to keep me amused for as long as I can imagine.*

In fact, I could barely remember the last time I'd touched a real person. As long as the VR designers kept these erotic episodes coming, I was perfectly happy to immerse myself in this dream world, where all of my wildest fantasies came true.

After my exciting Spring Break episode, I went home dreaming up my next fantasy escape at the virtual reality club. Each of my adventures had been more wild and interesting than the one before, and I began to wonder how I could possibly top the last one. Then it dawned on me that these were entirely *manufactured* scenes, and that theoretically I could custom-design virtually any scenario I wanted.

One of my longstanding fantasies had been to have sex with a celebrity, and the number one dreamboat on my list was the famous blond actor, Brad Whitt. I opened the Eros website and clicked on the program menu, typing in the actor's name in the search bar. Lo and behold, a CGI-generated character having a similar resemblance appeared on the screen with a short profile description:

Have you ever dreamed of meeting one of your favorite celebrities, close up? With our VIP simulation, you can have your choice of over one hundred movie stars, musicians, athletes, and other famous public figures. Brad Whitt has been the leading man in over fifty box office blockbusters. You can even drop yourself into one of his movies and play the role of one of his co-stars for a small bonus fee. Immerse yourself in the fantasy and imagine yourself playing opposite one of the sexiest movie stars of our generation!

Holy shit, I thought to myself, suddenly feeling my panties flooding with lubrication while I imagined myself co-starring with my idol, kissing him onscreen then having a secret tryst with him away from the camera. I immediately signed up for another session, and when I strapped myself into the virtual reality suit and the robotic chair the following day, I quickly scrolled through the menu, selecting the Brad Whitt program and his film *Mr. and Mrs. Jones.* I chose to play the role of his wife in the movie, the real-life Evangelista Jolie, then I requested the episode start with the famous scene of the two of them in their kitchen, having a sexy dinner together when their peaceful meal is interrupted by a home invasion of ninja-clad assassins.

The scene opened with the two of us sitting at opposing ends of a long table illuminated with romantic candles, eating a gourmet dinner and sipping wine.

"How was your day today, dear?" Brad Whitt's character asked me with his trademark dazzling smile.

"Oh, uh..." I stammered, trying to imagine myself in the role while I gazed into his smoldering eyes. "You know, same old, same old. Lots of boring meetings and dull reports. How about you?"

"Pretty much the same," Brad nodded. "More insuffer-able sales calls and client proposals. We really should look into getting more interesting jobs some day."

Unbeknownst to each of the main characters in the movie, the married couple were actually both government agents working independently as undercover assassins, eliminating international criminals while officially working at boring day jobs. Their real jobs were so secret, they were barred from even telling their *spouses* what they did behind the scenes.

"Yes," I smiled back at him, beginning to lose myself in the role while I crossed my legs under the table, trying to quell the rivers of fluid dribbling down the inside of my pantyhose. "I wish they'd let me out of the office once in a while to do some field work. At least *you* get to meet actual customers to break the monotony."

"Yeah, but my clients are so lame," Brad rolled his eyes, playing the role of disenchanted salesman to the hilt. "It's so easy to close the sale, they're such *lay-downs*."

"Well don't worry, sweetheart," I grinned. "I promise to make you work *harder* for it after we finish dinner. I won't be such an easy lay-down for you."

"Oh?" he smiled, taking a sip of his wine while he peered over the rim with a raised eyebrow. "We'll have to see about that–"

Suddenly, there was a creak in one of the floorboards in the nearby living room, and a bullet whizzed over the table, slicing one of the candles in half and denting the door of the kitchen's stainless steel fridge.

"Duck!" Brad said, flipping over the table, sending the dishes and cutlery clambering onto the floor.

He tapped one of the floorboards, and a hidden compartment popped up, revealing a shiny nine millimeter handgun. He grabbed the pistol grip and peered over the edge of the table, firing a perfectly aimed shot to drop one of the black-coated intruders. Shortly after, a series of machine gun shots hammered across the front of the table, and we scampered over to the side of the fridge, opening the door as a barrier against the fusillade of bullets.

"Wait here," Brad said, placing his arms around my shoulders and giving me a kiss on my cheek. "I'll draw their fire while you run into the garage. Start up the Volvo, and I'll meet you there in a few minutes."

"Fuck *that*," I said, remembering how his screen wife had fought alongside him in the scene to protect them from the team of thugs, demonstrating equal finesse and skill in eliminating the invaders.

I reached up onto the kitchen counter toward the stash of chef's knives nestled in a wooded rack and pulled out two sharp blades, flinging them expertly in the direction of the advancing thugs, felling them with one dagger to the throat and another to the middle of his chest. Brad looked at me with a surprised expression, and I peered back at him with a sly smile.

"Looks like you're not the *only* one with a boring day job," I nodded. "It seems we do more than file boring reports and sell industrial machinery."

"I can't believe you've been holding back on me all this time!" he said with an exaggerated frown.

"*You're* the one who said he had to attend another boring out-of-town sales conference," I said, punching him in the shoulder.

"We'll talk about this later," he said, slamming the fridge door in the opposite direction to knock another assassin over as the team began to close in on us. "Right now, we need to get out of here. Are you ready to make a run for it?"

"Yeah," I huffed, grabbing a few extra knives from the rack as we prepared to dash toward the door leading to the garage.

"Okay," he said. "On three. One–"

Suddenly, I leapt to my feet, somersaulting over the overturned table, kicking one intruder in the face and slicing another's throat as I dropped three more assailants while Brad followed close behind, firing his pistol in rapid succession to keep the other intruders at bay. When we opened the garage door, we quickly swung it closed behind us as a cannonade of bullets slammed against the panel, then we started up the car with Brad in the driver's seat as he tossed me his pistol. We didn't even bother trying to retract the front door of the garage, slamming through it with splintering wood and squealing down the driveway, screeching our tires onto the side street as a train of black SUVs followed close behind in rapid pursuit.

While a spray of bullets slammed against the back of our car and shattered the back window, Brad careened the car from side to side to avoid oncoming traffic, looking at me with a disgruntled frown.

"Can you do something about that?" he said, looking at me like this whole thing was somehow all my fault.

"I'll see what I can do," I huffed, turning around and kneeling on my seat cushion while I pointed the Beretta at the column of cars following us, shooting out their tires and making them tumble end-over-end and slam into other cars parked at the side of the street.

"Better," he nodded, peering into the rear-view mirror as we began to put some extra distance between our followers.

Suddenly, he drifted the back end of the Volvo into a side-skid while he turned around a corner, noticing a nearby underground garage, and he slammed the car onto the angled entranceway, jumping the car over the closed gate and squealing to a stop in a vacant spot near the opposite end of the garage. We waited a few moments while we listened to see if any of our followers had noticed us duck into the garage, then when we heard the the cars screaming past us down the street, we turned to peer at one another with sheepish smiles.

"Good work," Brad said, reaching out to squeeze my hand.

"You're not so bad, yourself," I smiled, leaning over to kiss him on the cheek.

He grabbed my ass and pulled me overtop of him, with me straddling his hips away from the camera perched on the front hood of our car, kissing me passionately while our car purred softly in the quiet underground cavern.

"So, what do we do now?" Brad said, referring to our newly exposed lives and seemingly burned status as government agents.

"I guess we're going to have to rely on *ourselves* from now on," I grinned while unzipping his pants and reaching into his trousers. "But first, there was that little matter of the lay-down that we discussed earlier..."

Even though the camera was still rolling and the following scene in the movie almost certainly involved the two actors *simulating* sex while they rocked their hips together and moaned into each other's mouths, there was nothing stopping me from play-acting this for all it was worth in the privacy of my VR suit and locked cubicle. I reached into Brad's pants and pulled out his hardening tool, lifting up my dress while I angled my steaming pussy over his bobbing cock, slowly lowering myself over his thick pole. I had no way of knowing if the specifications of his virtual reality avatar matched his real-life stats, but the length and girth of his stiff cock stretched me to my fullest capacity while he slowly filled me up.

"Mmm," I groaned into his mouth as he sunk his dick all

the way into my throbbing hole. "That's quite a weapon you were hiding from me..."

"You mean the *Beretta* under the kitchen floorboards?"

"Among other things," I grinned, rocking my ass slowly over his hips as his big tool slid effortlessly inside my dripping pussy.

"Yeah, well, I didn't know you had such an affinity for long, hard objects..."

"Are you referring to the kitchen knives?" I grinned.

"Among other things," he grunted, placing his hands over the back of my ass and pulling my hips harder over his burning erection.

I knew that he was imagining himself making love to his *real-life* wife in the scene and that the camera was still rolling as the film director looked on from his remote studio while the camera on the front of our car filmed us through the windshield, but it hardly mattered. In the fantasy cocoon of the virtual reality studio, I was sitting in the lap of my favorite movie star, fucking him hard while he gazed back into my eyes and kissed me passionately, 'pretending' to make love to me while the camera still rolled, showing only our upper bodies.

"We better put on a good show for the camera," he whispered into my ear as he humped me with his big dick. "No need to rush things..."

"Not at all," I grunted back in his ear. "We need to make this look as authentic as possible."

"Damn, girl," he hissed as he flexed his buttock muscles, driving his tool up and down into my dripping hole. "You're *full* of surprises today. What are you doing after the scene wraps and we go home for the day?"

"I dunno," I rasped, grinding my pussy over his hard mound as my juices dripped down between his legs and over his tightening balls. "We never properly finished that dinner earlier..."

"Mmm, I'd like that," he nodded. "I've got something special in mind for dessert–"

"Oh?" I said, raising an eyebrow as we both peered at one another with reddening cheeks. "Better than *this*?"

"You have no idea," he grunted, digging his fingers into my ass as he angled his hips forward, preparing to come inside my throbbing pussy. "There are so many more things I want to do to you when the camera stops rolling."

"I like the sound of that," I shuddered, feeling my pleasure overtaking me as I gushed into his lap and he jerked his hips against me while we groaned into each other's mouths.

19

———————

As eager as I was to continue my fantasy adventure with Brad Whitt, I wanted to use the remaining hour of my scheduled session to experience the *other* half of my dream celebrity matchup, a secret tryst with his hot real-life wife, Evangelista Jolie. One of my favorite movies starring her was the film *Girl, Imprisoned*, in which she plays a mental patient locked up in a hospital with the equally lithesome actress Winnie Rider. The two form a special bond rebelling against the system, with the main protagonist eventually finding freedom and absolution when she's released from the institution many months later.

I paused the Brad Whitt simulation and reprogrammed the system to drop me into the movie playing the role of Winnie Rider, shortly after she'd been admitted to the hospital. My first scene involved meeting with the hospital psychiatrist, and after fast-forwarding through the boring discussion of my troubled past and expectations for treatment in the hospital, I was admitted by the head nurse and escorted to my sleeping quarters. Evangelista Jolie's character was lazily propped up on the opposite bunk, reading a girlie magazine with one knee angled upward, revealing her tight ass in her hospital-issued jumpsuit.

"Hi," I said after the nurse left me alone in the room, dropping my duffel bag next to my small cot.

"Hey," Evangelista said, peering nonchalantly over the top of her magazine.

I unpacked my belongings, carefully stowing them in the upright dresser resting next to my bed, feeling the eyes of my roommate running her eyes over my body while she sized me up.

"So what are you in for?" she said, dropping her magazine into her lap.

"Trying to *kill* myself," I smiled, peering back at her over my shoulder. "Or so they think. I just took a few too many sleeping pills."

"So you weren't actually trying to off yourself?"

"No, I just wanted to dull the pain a little..."

"Troubled home life?" my new roommate said.

"Something like that. Absentee father and overbearing mother–"

"Been there, done that," Evangelista nodded.

"What's *your* crime?" I said.

"Beating up a kid at school then running away from home when I was thirteen."

"That sounds pretty normal," I said, noticing the darting of her orange uniform from the actress's famously pointy breasts.

"Yeah, except I did it *three times*. Apparently, you're not considered capable of making important decisions until you're an adult in America."

"And you thought you were an adult at the age of *thirteen*?" I said, pinching my brows together.

"I was an early bloomer," Evangelista said. "And lots

more mature than most of my peers. I think I could have made a go of it if I'd gotten far enough away–"

"So your parents stuck you in here to avoid having to deal with you?"

"Yup," she nodded. "Story of my life."

"Sounds familiar," I said, peering around the starkly furnished room. "So, what do people do for fun around here? The common area was filled with a bunch of catatonic patients peering out the window and building jigsaw puzzles–"

"Most of these shut-ins are pretty fucked up," Evangelista nodded. "They'll just make you more depressed if you hang around them."

Then she hopped off her bed and grabbed my hand, pulling me toward the entrance of our room and peering around the side of the doorjamb.

"Come on," she said, pulling me down a vacant hallway. "I know somewhere we can be alone."

She dragged me into a utility room then pulled some hairpins out of her side pocket, inserting them into a locked door on the other end of the closet.

"Where does that go?" I said, peering at the steel door.

"To the underground tunnels," she smiled. "It's mostly filled with sewers and pipes, but at least we won't have any nurses or orderlies keeping an eye on us."

She twisted the pins in the lock socket, then she swung open the door, signaling for me to enter the darkened cavern.

"Where did you learn to do that?" I said, widening my eyes at how easily she'd bypassed the hospital's security systems.

"On the *streets*, where else? You have to learn how to live by your wits and the tips of your fingernails when you're all alone at such a tender age."

I scrunched my face into an uncomfortable grimace when I smelt the foul odor from the basement wafting over my nose.

"Are you sure this place is *safe*?" I said, peering into the dusky tunnel. "What if we can't get out?"

"I know an exit on the other side," Evangelista nodded, grabbing my hand. "Don't worry, I know this place like the back of my hand by now. You only live once. Let's break the rules and live on our *own* terms for a change."

"Okay..." I said, reluctantly following her down the rickety stairs into a dark passageway with a brackish stream running down the middle of the tunnel.

"Are those *rats*?" I said, suddenly stopping and pressing myself against the concrete wall while a column of rodents scurried along the opposite wall.

"Yeah, but they'll leave you alone as long as you don't get in their way..."

"Which way is *that*, exactly?" I said, pressing my body closer to hers for protection.

"Close to *me*, of course," she smiled.

"I can do that," I nodded, squeezing her hand tightly.

She turned toward me and pressed her hips against mine, pinning me against the wall while she peered into my eyes in the misty darkness, feeling my cold breath on her cheeks.

"Have you had sex before?" she said, grinding her mound against me.

"A couple of times with one of the boys at my high school," I grunted. "But it didn't last very long."

"Boys have no clue what to do with girls at that age," Evangelista said, unzipping my tunic and slipping one hand under my bra, squeezing my breast. "Only a *woman* knows how to properly satisfy another woman."

"Oh?" I said, playing the role of the naive, innocent girl. "Do you have *experience* with that sort of thing?"

"Plenty," she smiled, pinching my nipple and rolling it softly between her fingers. "You've got to find *something* to do to keep yourself amused in this all-girl institution."

"Mmm," I grunted, feeling my panties moistening as Evangelista's rosebud lips pressed against my mouth. "I like the feel of your fingers on my skin."

"Maybe you'll like it even more if I go a little *lower*," she grinned, tracing a line down the middle of my stomach with the tip of her finger.

"Yes," I panted, tilting my hips upward to meet her drifting hand, hardly believing I was the object of attention with one of the planet's sexiest female movie stars, albeit in a fantasy film sequence.

"Do you *like* that?" she said, tilting her head to the side of my cheek and teasing the rim of my ear with her outstretched tongue.

"Yes," I groaned, feeling her fingers slip under the band of my panties and over the warm fur covering my mound.

Normally, I shaved my mound bare before having sex with anyone, but the role of my character was an eighteen-year-old inexperienced mental patient, and I reveled in the feeling of my scene-generated muff bristling while she teased me with the tips of her fingers.

"Does your boyfriend at school do *this* to you when he makes love to you?" she whispered into my ear.

"No," I shuddered, rocking my hips while I encouraged her to go lower. "He usually goes straight for the bull's-eye and sticks his fingers inside my hole."

"That's not where most of the *good* stuff is," Evangelista

said, sticking her tongue into my ear while she drifted her hand under the curve of my mound, softly circling my slippery clit. "Does he know where to find your magic *button*?"

"Hell, no," I hissed while she massaged my hardening gland. "He's only interested in one thing, getting his rocks off as fast as he can."

"That's a shame," Evangelista murmured. "Because you're quite a dish. He doesn't know what he's missing, taking the time to savor all your trimmings and garnishes."

"Yes," I rasped, feeling my pleasure building inexorably as she expertly teased and manipulated my clit. "That feels so good..."

"You're so soft and wet," she nodded. "I can't wait to feel your naked body pressed up against mine when we get back to our room."

"Why don't we go *now*?" I said, sucking her puffy lip into my mouth while she danced her tongue with mine. "I'd love to rub my pussy against the *rest* of your pretty body–"

"Soon enough," Evangelista smiled, circling her fingers harder over my nub while she fucked my mouth with her tongue.

"Oh God," I rasped, feeling my pleasure reaching the bursting point.

I clamped my thighs tightly around her hand and titled my hips upward, jerking my pussy over her fingers while gushing my juices over her arm and my one-piece hospital uniform.

"Holy *shit*," she said, flaring her eyes open in surprise. "You can squirt! I have got to get me some more of this before we go down for the night."

She held me in her arms until I stopped shaking, then she slowly retracted her hand from my jumpsuit, running her dripping fingers around the edges of my mouth while I nibbled on them softly.

"Let's get the fuck out of here," she said, grabbing my hand and pulling me along the narrow passageway back in the direction of the utility closet. "There's something *else* I want you to squirt on that's been feeling a little neglected lately..."

20

―――――

When we got back into the utility room and locked the passageway door behind us, she cracked open the front door and twisted her head to peer down the hall. When she saw that the way was clear, she pulled my hand and we scurried down the hallway giggling like little girls, slipping back into our shared room, closing the door behind us. Soon after, there was a loud beeping sound over the p.a. system, and our door locked automatically from the outside while all the lights went out in our room.

"Jesus," I said, peering around the darkness, trying to adjust my eyes. "These guys don't fool around, do they? Is this place *always* locked up so tight?"

"Only during sleeping hours," Evangelista nodded. "But it's just as well. It's the only time we have complete privacy and autonomy. They have no idea what goes on behind closed doors when everybody is supposedly resting."

"I can imagine," I said, squeezing Evangelista's moist fingers. "But I'd rather not imagine. I'd rather feel your sexy body next to mine."

"You don't have to ask twice, girl," Evangelista said, pulling me toward her small bunk in the opposite corner and unzipping my pantsuit, pulling it down over my ankles. I did the same with hers, then we quickly pulled off each other's bras and panties, tumbling into her cot and banging our heads softly against the concrete wall.

"There's not a lot of room to maneuver on these little beds," she said, intertwining her legs with mine while we rubbed our chilly tits together.

"How do you want to do this?" I said, eager to feel her warm pussy pressing up against me.

"Why don't you lie down while I sit on top of you?" she said. "That way, I can look at you from the dim light coming through the window and I can teach you how a woman makes love to another woman..."

"Yes, please," I panted, prostrating myself on the bed and pretending to play the role of a lesbian virgin, even though I'd experienced more than my share of girl-on-girl sex previously.

But never with the queen of modern-day movie starlets, I thought to myself. *Who every teenage boy and half the planet's red-blooded women had dreamed of rolling in the sack with.*

"You're beautiful," Evangelista said, kneeling over my pinned hips with her moist pussy as she stared down at me in the moonlit room, running the palms of her hands up my trembling abdomen.

"You look incredible in this light," I nodded, staring at her upright, pointed breasts and the narrow indentation running down the center of her ripped stomach toward the dark triangle between her legs.

Having never seen her real tits completely uncovered in any of her movies, I couldn't stop staring at her magnificent melons, reaching out to caress them softly and pinching her impossibly long and hard nipples.

"Mmm," she groaned while she cupped my breasts, squeezing them firmly while she rocked her snatch over my mound, soaking my pubic hairs with her dripping pussy. "You're soft everywhere–"

"Not *everywhere*," I smiled, tilting my hips upward into her warm pocket, feeling her juices dribbling over my twitching clit.

"I want to feel that beautiful pussy of yours again," she nodded, raising up her hips and pressing my legs apart while she pulled one of my legs forward. "Except this time, with a *different* part of my anatomy. Let's see how much you like being fucked by a *woman,* instead of a boy's impatient dick..."

"I'm already enjoying it a thousand times more," I grunted, tilting my hips to meet hers as she swiveled her slit against mine, scissoring our vulvas together.

"Yes, baby," Evangelista groaned, grinding her pussy against mine. "Fuck me with that juicy pussy. I want to feel you gushing all over my *cunt* this time when you come."

"Mhhhh," I hissed, staring at her bouncing, pointed breasts while our connected pussies began to slurp from our grinding labia. "I think that can be arranged..."

"Fuck, this is hot," she panted, staring down at me with a flushed face. "I'm so turned on from fingering you downstairs, I'm ready to come anytime. Are you going to come with me?"

"Yes," I grunted, grabbing the sides of her buttocks and pulling our pussies harder together.

When she felt our nubs sliding over one another, she titled her head upwards in a fit of ecstasy, squeezing my tits so hard I thought they might burst, then she growled a deep groan, shaking her hips rapidly against mine while her upper body convulsed in synchronized pleasure. It took her almost a full minute to come down from her orgasm, then she peered down at me with a confused expression.

"You didn't *squirt* on me this time," she said, shaking her head in dismay. "Weren't you able to come?"

"I could have," I smiled back at her. "But there's something I've been fantasizing about doing with you pretty much from the moment I laid eyes on you. Do you mind if we switch positions while I finish myself off? There's another part of your body I've been dying to squirt on for the longest time–"

"Okay," Evangelista said, tumbling down beside me and turning over onto her back. "But I thought you said you were inexperienced with girls..."

"I didn't say that exactly," I smiled as I rolled over on top of her, shimmying my hips higher up on her stomach. "I just said that I'd had sex with inexperienced boys."

"Okay," she nodded, feeling my wet pussy leaving a trail of juices up the indentation of her flexing abdomen. "If you want me to suck your pussy when you come this time, I'm happy to have you squirt all over my face."

"I was thinking of a *different* part of your body," I grinned, positioning my dripping snatch overtop one of her pointed breasts and still-erect nipples, lowering myself down over her firm flesh and squashing it like a pancake.

"Mmft," she grunted, struggling to catch her breath as I pressed my weight on top of her. "I've never been *tit-fucked* before–"

"Then you don't know what you're missing," I smiled, rocking my wet pussy on her breast while I felt her hard teat slipping in and out of my dripping slit. "And neither do your *partners*, because that's one of your best features."

"Mmm," she nodded, grunting louder as I rocked my hips harder over her heaving chest. "I like the feeling of this. I'm definitely going to add this to my repertoire of girl-on-girl sex in the future."

"You should," I grunted, feeling my orgasm welling up inside me as my pussy sloshed against her wet skin. "Did you know some women can orgasm simply by having their *nipples* stimulated? It's not uncommon for nursing mothers to climax while their babies suckle on their tits..."

"You sure know a lot about women's sexuality for someone who's led a supposedly suppressed life."

"Yeah," I groaned, feeling my floodgates about to burst. "But I have a pretty active fantasy life. And I've watched a lot of movies, dreaming about making love to a lot of sexy women."

"Oh my God," Evangelista said, flaring her eyes open in growing pleasure. "I can feel it coming again. Come *with* me this time. I want to watch you gushing all over my tits while we climax together–"

"*Fuck* yes," I grunted, spreading my knees further apart as I spilled over the tipping point. "I'm *coming*, baby. I'm coming all over your amazing tits..."

While I gushed a veritable geyser over Evangelista's heaving chest, sending jets of fluid squirting in every direction, she spread her lips apart, trying to catch as much of my spray as she could in her gaping mouth as she lifted her hips off the mattress, coming simultaneously with me while we stared into each other's eyes, each of us living a fantasy neither one of us imagined was previously possible. We jerked our bodies together for the longest time, savoring the feeling of our warm, dripping skin meshing together, then I flopped onto the mattress beside her, caressing the tops of her upturned breasts softly with the back of my hand.

"Thank you, Eros," I muttered softly, staring up at the ceiling while I paid homage to the modern-day technology of virtual reality.

"Who?" Evangelista said, turning her head to peer at me with a wrinkled forehead.

"It's nothing," I sighed. "Just thanking the goddess of love for the miracle of bringing us together."

"Yeah," Evangelista gushed. "Who would have thought that two fucked-up girls would find so much happiness stuck together in a mental institution?"

21

After our hot dorm scene wrapped, Evangelista and I went to a local restaurant for supper, where we discussed our private lives and future film projects. It was kind of fun playing the role of the pretty actress Winnie Rider, who I'd also had a crush on when I was younger, and it was hard to concentrate on eating while I gawked at Evangelista's pretty face and figure.

"That last scene was pretty hot," she said while slurping spaghetti from her plate into her puffy, red lips.

"Yeah," I nodded, feeling my panties still dripping from the last episode. "Do you think theater goers will know that we were having actual sex below the view of the camera focusing on our upper bodies?"

"I don't know," she smiled. "But I bet my *husband* will be suspicious when he sees the final take."

"Brad?" I said, reluctant to tell her about my equally hot sex scene from the movie Mr. and Mrs. Jones. "You two are like Hollywood royalty. I can't imagine him being jealous of you starring alongside any other actor."

"This one might be a little different," she frowned. "You two used to *date* for a while in a previous life, didn't you?"

"Only briefly," I nodded, remembering how the two stars had a short fling from the gossip magazines. "But it never amounted to anything serious..."

"Still, he talks about you frequently. I can tell he still has fond memories."

"Yeah, but now he's got the sexiest movie star in the world as his wife–"

"It's not as perfect as it sounds," Evangelista said. "I think he misses those carefree days when he could sow his wild oats with whomever he wanted."

"Do you ever feel the same temptations?" I said.

"Fuck, yeah," she nodded. "That's one of the good things about being an actor. You can lose yourself in another romantic fantasy every couple of months with a new sexy partner and some pretend sex scenes–"

"Or *not* so pretend," I chuckled.

"Yes," she sighed.

Evangelista paused for a moment, staring down at her plate while she twirled another strand of noodles around her fork.

"Why don't you come over to *our* place for dinner sometime?" she said, suddenly looking up.

I paused for a moment while I peered at her with a surprised expression.

"You don't think that might be a bit awkward?"

"Maybe at first," she said. "But I'm sure it wouldn't take long for Brad to warm up to the idea. Who knows, maybe we could even relive some of our private moments together by sharing a little three-way *dessert*..."

"Akk," I suddenly choked on my seared scallops, imagining having sex with my two favorite movie stars at the same time. "Do you think he'd *go* for that?"

"I'm pretty sure, if we *teased* him enough," she nodded. "But we might have to put on a bit of a show to demonstrate we're okay with it..."

"That could be kind of fun," I grinned, squeezing my thighs together under the table to keep my juices from dribbling all the way down the insides of my pants.

"It's a date, then," Evangelista smiled. "I'll send you a text with all the details. Keep the kettle boiling."

"Oh, it's boiling, alright," I grunted. "In fact, it's almost ready to *spill over...*"

~

In the next frame of my VR scenario, I received a note from Evangelista, and I squirmed in my tight bodysuit, barely able to contain my excitement.

It's all set, she typed. *Meet us this Thursday at nine. Come wearing something sexy...*

"Holy fuck!" I grunted in my fogging helmet. "Is this really happening? I'm going to have sex with Brad Whitt and Evangelista Jolie *at the same time?*"

I quickly replied to her message, then the VR program took me to the front doorstep of their palatial Hollywood Hills estate, where I rang the doorbell, staring up at the security camera over the door like a deer caught in the headlights.

Evangelista opened the door then she glanced down at my tight, black dress with a plunging neckline and long zipper running up the back.

"Hi," I smiled, staring at her sexy Oscar de la Renta designed pantsuit. "It's good to see you again."

"It's good to see you too," she said, grabbing my hand and pulling me into their marble-floored foyer. "I'm glad you could make our little date."

"I wouldn't miss it for the world," I said. "Do you think I'm dressed appropriately?"

"It's perfect," she nodded, glancing down at my plump breasts, pushed up by an underwire bra.

She led me into their enormous living room overlooking the valley, where Brad was sitting on their designer sofa, reading a trade magazine. He stood up when he saw me, and walked over next to the two of us, giving me a soft kiss on the cheek.

"Nice to see you again, Winnie," he smiled with his perfect teeth. "It's been a while."

"Too long," I nodded, noticing a slight bulge in his tight-fitting dress pants.

"Would you like an aperitif before dinner?" Evangelista said, smiling at my flushed face.

"That would be lovely," I said, trying not to stare at Brad's carved chest muscles peeking out of his partially unbuttoned silk shirt.

"Aperol?" she said, heading toward the kitchen.

"Perfect," I said, standing awkwardly beside Brad with my hands crossed in front of my dress.

"How've you been?" he said, motioning for me to make myself comfortable on their large sectional sofa. "I hear you and Ang are making a movie together."

"Yes," I said, blushing a deeper shade of red. "It's a bit dark, but I think it might be a winner."

"I'm sure it will be, with the two of you playing the lead roles. How are you finding Angie to work with?"

"She's a dream," I said, crossing my legs to highlight my gym-toned calves. "She's such a great actress, she'll probably walk away with all the awards at the next Golden Globes."

"She's got enough of those, already," Brad laughed, peering up at the fireplace mantel where their combined acting awards shone in the setting sun. "You're long overdue."

"Thanks," I said, trying not to flash back to our previous on-set fling to keep my dress dry.

Evangelista reentered the room, carrying the pink cocktail, then she handed it to me while smiling at her husband.

"The staff have got dinner ready," she said to me. "Are you hungry?"

"Famished," I said. "My mouth has been watering all day."

"Glad to hear," Evangelista said, motioning for the two of us to follow her into their palatial dining room. "Our chef has prepared a five-course meal. I hope there's enough to sate your appetite."

"I'm sure there will be," I smiled, staring at their rock-hard asses while the sexy couple walked hand-in-hand toward their parlor.

I paused for a moment, staring at their impeccably arranged table with ten upholstered chairs positioned around the perimeter, reminding me of the sexy scene in Brad's movie where we'd flirted at opposite ends of the long table before the invasion of assassins.

"Why don't you sit at the head of the table?" Brad said, seeming to read my mind. "That way, Angie and I can sit on opposite sides of you while we get caught up."

"Okay," I said as Brad pulled out my chair and I sat carefully in the plush chair so as not to rip my tight dress.

The servers soon after brought out the first course of beet-red soup, placing the steaming bowls in front of each of our place settings, and Brad stirred his broth with a spoon while he peered across the table at his sexy wife.

"Winnie tells me you've been stealing all the good scenes in your latest movie," he grinned, obviously trying to stir up more than just the soup.

"I wouldn't go *that* far," Evangelista grinned. "She's had some pretty intense moments, herself."

"I hear the sex scenes are making insider tongues wag," he said, taking a sip of the steaming broth.

"Well, she's pretty hard to resist," Angie said, winking at me. "We have some good chemistry on screen..."

"What do *you* think, Winnie?" Brad said, turning toward me. "Have you been immersing yourself in the role?"

I lifted a spoonful of soup to my lips, stalling for an appropriate answer.

"It's been fun working with Angie," I nodded, taking a careful sip. "But you know, it's just acting..."

"And was all the *waterworks* just acting too?"

I suddenly choked on my soup, spilling the red liquid over the front of my dress, and Evangelista rose out of her seat, dipping her napkin into a glass of water, rubbing it over my breast, causing my nipple to harden and dart the front of my outfit.

"We should get you out of that dress to treat it before the stain sets in," she said, raising me out of my chair and unfastening the zipper running down the length of my dress, all the way down to my ass.

She peered at my lacy bra, noticing the stain had seeped through to my white undergarments, then she lowered her head, sucking on the stain while I arched my back, groaning softly.

"There's no need, Angie..." I protested, but Evangelista

seemed determined to titillate me in front of her husband while she buried her face deeper in my cleavage.

"This is going to require some heavier soaking," she said, reaching around to unclasp the back of my bra and hanging it over the back of the chair. "But let's get this sticky stuff off your *skin* first..."

She pressed me back down onto the chair with my dress draped over my hips, then she threaded her legs through the open armrests and squatted over my hips, sucking my nipples one after the other hard into her mouth, slurping on them loudly while she rocked her ass on my lap.

"Uhnnn," I groaned, moving my hips in tandem with her as I slid my fingers through her hair, pulling her head harder toward my chest.

"Is *this* more character acting?" Brad said, staring at the two of us making out while he squirmed in his chair.

"It never hurts to prepare for the next scene," Evangelista grinned, glancing at his tenting trousers while she circled my erect nipples with her darting tongue. "Perhaps you'd like to *direct* us. After all, I understand you have some prior experience in these matters also..."

"Mmm," he said, unzipping his pants and freeing his bobbing hard-on. "But I think we should repair to the boudoir to properly set the scene. I have a few ideas how we can add an extra element to raise the sexual tension a notch higher..."

22

————

Brad grabbed each of our hands and pulled us toward their sumptuous bedroom with an enormous, four-poster bed, then he slowly disrobed the two of us, caressing our naked bodies with the palms of his hands while we pulled down his pants, sliding our hands over his bobbing erection.

"It's been a while since we had our last threesome," Evangelista smiled at him. "How would you like to do it this time? Something tells me you've already been planning this scene."

"It's all I've been able to think about since I heard Winnie was coming over," he nodded, thrusting his dripping hard-on into our eager hands. "But I want to watch the two of you two *alone* first. Show me what you did out of view of the camera. I want to relive that moment when I watch the scene later."

"Mmm," Evangelista hummed, twisting my nipples while she glanced down at my dripping crotch. "Why don't I show you what I was thinking for our *next* scene? You might even be able to get into the action if you play your cards right..."

Angie pushed me gently down on top of the mattress, then she crawled overtop me, swinging her body around until we were in a sixty-nine position, staring at each other's wet slits.

"This is one thing we never got around to doing," she grinned, inhaling my musky scent. "I've tasted her juices before, but not while sucking her sweet pussy. Why don't you sit back and enjoy the show while you see what special tricks Winnie can cook up?"

"Yes," Brad said, pulling an armchair from the edge of the room closer to the side of the mattress to get a bird's-eye view of the action. "I remember well some of the tricks she performed during our previous time together..."

"I bet you *do*," Evangelista nodded, burying her head between my thighs and slurping up my juices while she lowered her hips onto my face.

I stuck my tongue into her hole and wrapped my arms around her flexing ass while she pressed her clit against my chin, humping my face as she sucked my jewel into her mouth while Brad watched on from his chair, fapping his hard-on as he took in the action. I couldn't see much with Angie's thighs locked around my head, but the thought of him ogling my dripping pussy while his wife ate me out was enough to send rivers of lubrication dripping down the inside of my thighs.

"*That's* the Winnie I remember," he huffed, jerking his cock with two hands as he stared at my dripping labia and flexing buttocks.

"Are you just going to sit there and *watch* the whole time?" Evangelista teased. "I know you're dying to sink your dick into her again after all this time. Why don't you fuck her pretty pussy while I play with her clit? That is, if Winnie's game for a little repeat performance..."

"Fuck, yes," I grunted, tilting my hips upward to display my gaping slit. "I've dreamed about having the two of you together for the longest time."

"Well, here's your chance, sweetheart," Angie said, grinding her pussy against my face while Brad rose from his chair, sliding the tip of his cock down my folds as his wife stared at his flexing abs.

"Yes, baby," she purred, angling his tool into my hole. "Fuck Winnie's sweet pussy while I watch her squirt on your balls. You're not the *only* one who's been fantasizing about what she could do with the two of us once we all got together."

"Unghh," Brad groaned as he slid his dick into my crevasse. While he started to rock his hips back and forth, Evangelista turned her head to the side, sucking my gland into her puffy lips as her husband slid his glistening shaft against the side of her cheeks.

"Fuck, this is so hot," she groaned, sucking on my bean harder. "It's too bad our new movie features only *women*. You could inject some much-needed testosterone into the equation."

"That's not the *only* thing I'd like to inject into the equation," Brad grunted, slapping his cock against my dripping cunt and his wife's flushing face at the same time.

"I'm going to come soon," I hissed from the other edge of the bed while darting my tongue over Angie's hardening nub. "This is too much, I can't hold it much longer..."

"Let it rip, Win," Evangelista said, reaching behind her husband's flexing buttocks to squeeze his tightening balls. "It feels like Brad's ready to let go any time now."

"Oh fuck, oh fuck–" I groaned, feeling my orgasm coming on like a freight train. "You both feel so good–"

Seconds later, I erupted like Mount Vesuvius, gushing

my juices all over Angie's face and Brad's pulsing balls while he emptied his seed inside my pussy and Angie flapped her thighs against my head while we all climaxed together. It was the most exciting thing I'd ever experienced, and while we all shook our bodies together, I clamped my pussy tightly over Brad's throbbing dick and circled my arms around Angie's flexing hips, not wanting to let either of them go. But moments later, my VR session faded to black, and I lay in my vibrating chair and dripping suit, panting in satisfaction from the most erotic fantasy I'd ever experienced.

23

———————

I went home after finishing my latest VR session, thinking I couldn't possibly top that last episode. After all, what could be more thrilling than imagining yourself having sex with your favorite movie stars in a super-realistic fantasy chamber, where all of your senses were stimulated like you were actually there? But the more I thought about my simulated adventures and my discussions with the club's hostess Jillian, I began to realize there was still one thing missing. I was craving the human touch, the two-way interaction of real people turning each other on while they experienced one another's genuine reactions in real time. The cocoon of the virtual reality suit was really nothing more than a form of self-stimulated *porn*, albeit one with amazing 3-D imagery and surround sound.

I decided to go back into the club one last time and share my impressions with the pretty hostess, with a view to improving the experience for the next generation of users. When she saw me enter the facility, she came out into the lobby to greet me immediately, curious why I hadn't booked another session for some time.

"Hi Jade," she said, placing her hand on my elbow in the familiar way friends often do. "I noticed you haven't been into the studio in quite a while. Have you run out of fantasy scenarios to stimulate your interest and other body parts?"

"Not really," I smiled. "They've all been incredible, and I've scrolled through your online menu, finding plenty of other simulations that look interesting..."

"What's been holding you back from booking another session? I can offer you a special *discount* if you'd like. Lord knows, you've *earned* it with all the sessions you've booked so far."

"I actually had an idea how you could take the experience to the next level, if you've got a few minutes to listen to my proposal."

"Of course," she said, motioning for me to join her in her private office. "We get some of our best ideas for new programs from our customers. I'd love to hear your input."

When we got into her office, instead of sitting behind her desk like she usually did, she invited me to make myself comfortable on her small office sofa, where she joined me on the opposite side, crossing her legs with her raised foot only a few inches away from my knee.

"So what were you thinking?" she said, tapping her foot with a spiked heel playfully in my direction. "A different kind of setting? New characters? Some kinky new positions?"

"Something a little more *realistic*," I said, glancing at her sexy foot.

"I don't know how we can make it any more realistic without putting real people in the room with you. We've already created three-dimensional imagery, a special chair to simulate actual movement, and unique probes and sensors in the full-body suit to stimulate all of your senses–"

"I know," I said, crossing my own legs to face her more directly. "And all of that's fantastic. It's just, I'm missing the interaction of a *real person*..."

Jillian paused for a moment, pinching her eyebrows together uncomfortably.

"We're not set up for that sort of thing," she said. "This is a virtual reality club, using the latest technology to *simulate* real-world settings."

"Yes, I know," I nodded. "But what if we could simulate the look and feel of a real person, someone we *know*..."

"I'm pretty sure our lawyers wouldn't let us do that, with all the controversy over the privacy rights of individuals–"

"But you already have programs running simulations of famous *movie stars*."

"That's different," she said. "We have their approval to use their likeness if we share a percentage of the user fees each time someone includes them in one of their simulations."

"Couldn't we do something similar with other people we know?"

"I suppose it could be possible with *spouses* if we had their approval and a signed waiver–"

"I was thinking of somebody *else*," I smiled, grazing the tip of her shoe with my bouncing leg.

"Such as...?" Jillian said, sitting up higher in the sofa while she spread her knees slightly apart.

I hesitated for a moment then I pulled out my phone, tapping in the web address for the Eros website and scrolling to the staff profile page.

"Someone like *this*," I said, tapping on Jillian's picture and turning the screen around to show her.

Her eyes popped open and she blushed slightly, adjusting her position on the sofa again. But this time, I noticed a slight wet spot in the crotch of her pants, and she clamped her legs closed in embarrassment.

"Oh," she said, crossing her arms defensively over her billowing chest while she tried not to look at me. "What exactly would you have this, um, *avatar* do, assuming she agreed to participate in your simulated experience?"

"Well," I said, staring down at her moist crotch, partially concealed by her trembling legs. "I've spent quite a few lonely nights fantasizing about watching her in her office while she's viewing her computer screen–"

"*And?*" she said, beginning to relax her body posture as she peered into my eyes.

"I'd ask her to part her legs, then show me what she's watching on the screen..."

"What if I told you I was tapping into your *video feed* while you were watching all those sexy programs?"

"Then I'd ask her to unbutton her pants and show me what she did while she watched me enjoying those scenarios..."

"Like *this*?" she said, spreading her legs apart to reveal the large wet spot in her crotch as she slowly unbuttoned the top of her slacks.

"Yes," I purred, squirming my ass on the sofa while I watched her slipping her fingers under the waistband of her panties.

"What *else* would you want her to do in this simulated fantasy of yours?" she grunted, rolling her fingers slowly over her clit in her tight pants.

"I'd want her to take off the rest of her clothes and spread her legs far apart so I could stare at her pretty pussy while she stimulated herself watching me."

Jillian paused for a moment as she ran her eyes over my sexy figure with my hardening nipples.

"Well, it seems only fair that you do the same thing, since I'm not actually watching you in a simulated scenario right now..."

"Mmm," I said, standing up and taking off my clothes and throwing them on the floor before sitting back down on the sofa, facing her directly while I pulled the bottom of her pant legs, dragging her trousers down her legs as she unbuttoned her blouse and unclasped her bra. After we threw her clothes on top of mine, she raised her hips and pulled off her panties, throwing them onto the pile also.

"You know," she smiled, turning her naked body to face mine while spreading her legs slowly apart. "This isn't so far off my actual experience. I've fantasized more times than I can count about watching you enjoying some of those sexy programs while sitting at my desk alone."

"Oh?" I said, drifting my hands over my bare tits and circling my nipples with the tips of my fingers. "And did you *touch* yourself while I was squirming in my vibrating suit?"

"Yes," Jillian said, mimicking my movement while she teased her nipples and peered down at my dripping slit.

I paused for a moment while I glanced at her with a raised eyebrow.

"Were you *actually* able to tap into my feed to see what I was watching?" I said.

"No, but I could easily imagine what you were doing based on the character selections you made and the scenarios you chose."

"Did it turn you on that I chose *lesbian* interactions for many of my scenarios?"

"Yes," she panted, drifting her hand down the front of her abdomen while she watched me do the same.

"What did you imagine I was doing with all those pretty

women while I was strapped into that probing suit and rocking chair?"

"I could only *dream*..." Jillian shuddered as her fingers slid over her shaved mound onto her glistening vulva.

"Well, you're not dreaming *now*," I smiled, inserting two fingers into my slit while tilting my hips upward to sink them all the way into my hole.

"No," she groaned, copying my action and sliding her fingers slowly in and out of her dripping pussy. "And I didn't even have to ask your permission..."

"Nor *yours*," I grunted, rocking my hips faster while I stared into her eyes, watching a flush beginning to creep up over her breasts and straining neck.

"Maybe we don't need to get the lawyers involved in your proposal after all," she smiled. "We can live out your fantasies in the privacy of our own bedrooms."

"Don't you want to know what I was doing with all those partners in my simulated fantasies?"

"Yes, but I'd rather play them out *live*, face to face and skin to skin..."

"And pussy to pussy?"

"Yes," Jillian groaned, shimmying her hips closer to mine while we parted our legs further apart and mashed our cunnies together.

"Is this your first time doing this with a *woman*?" I said, watching the look on her face as she stared with wide eyes between our legs at our grinding pussies.

"Yes," she said. "Unless you count all the times I've used the suit with my own special programs..."

"Mmm, you'll have to tell me about that sometime," I grunted, feeling the familiar pangs of an impending climax building up inside me. "Maybe we can share stories and create our *own* virtual reality scenario with the two of us acting out our mutual fantasies."

"Or we can do that right *here* instead," Jillian groaned, pressing her pussy against mine as her mouth began to gape open.

"I like that idea," I nodded, feeling myself about to fall over the precipice. "As long as you don't mind me making a mess of your pretty sofa."

I grabbed the sides of her hips and pulled her crotch harder against mine, then I arched my back, groaning loudly while I sprayed my juices over her flapping legs and shaking belly.

"Oh my God," she grunted when she felt me squirting on her pussy. "Is *that* what you've been doing all this time, making such a mess of our latex suit?"

"Yes," I shuddered, jerking my hips spastically as I slowly came down from my powerful orgasm.

"Well, fuck the *suit*," Jillian huffed, jerking her hips along with me. "I don't want to waste any of that lubrication on a bunch of plastic probes and sensors. I want to see where else you can shower me with your juices, *flesh to flesh*."

"I'm glad you asked," I said, crawling up over her dripping body and sliding my wet pussy up the front of her stomach. "Because I've got all *kinds* of fantasies I'd like to replay in your private office..."

Ready *for more erotic chills and thrills? Read the next exciting volume in Jade's Erotic Adventures, Glory Hole. Buy direct and save at victoriarusherotica. Or download from your favorite online bookstore here: retailer links.*

They say your other senses are heightened whenever one is turned off...

SNEAK PEEK - GLORY HOLE

Chapter 1

When I received another titillating invitation to a party at my friend Madison's house, I couldn't wait to open the message. She always hosted the most interesting and sexy events, and with the cryptic subject heading *Glory Hole*, I could already feel my heart pounding while I began to read the message.

Dear Jade,

You are cordially invited to a party at my place this Saturday evening, starting at 9 p.m.

As with my previous events, there will be an exciting game designed to loosen everyone's inhibitions and get our juices flowing.

I don't want to give too much away, except to say there'll be more than a few surprises behind the curtain.

So get ready to mix it up with friends and foes alike, because in this game, there's no telling who or how you'll be paired up.

Be there or be square,
Maddy
P.S.: Make sure you're scrubbed clean, and I do mean everywhere, because no area of your body will be off limits!

Holy cow, I thought after reading her message. *What in God's name has she dreamed up this time? No area off limits? Mixing it up with friends and foes? And what exactly was going to happen behind this so-called curtain?* I had no idea what she was planning, but she was right about one thing. It was already getting my juices flowing.

As my mind began to wander about the hijinks she had in store, my hand slipped under my panties, imagining who might be stimulating me through this mysterious glory hole...

When I arrived at Madison's house on the night of the party, she escorted me to her living room, where a group of guests sipped wine around the perimeter of a large, cube-shaped curtain hanging from her living room ceiling. In the middle of the curtain on each side, roughly at waist height, were circular cut-outs of six-inch diameter. Some of the guests playfully wagged their fingers through the holes, while others nodded knowingly, anticipating what Maddy had in store.

I recognized a few of the faces in the crowd, but there were also some new people I hadn't met before. With an even sprinkling of men and women, I scanned the group while everybody made small talk introducing themselves. On the women's side were my friends Emma, Bonnie, and

Lily from last summer's all-girl camping trip, plus Brad's hot wife Laura, the sexy African-Asian girl Mia, the full-figured redhead Paige, Lucas's pretty girlfriend Amy, and the trans-gender cabaret singer Shae. But standing next to Shae was a new woman I hadn't seen before. Tall and statuesque with a body to die for, she and Shae were rubbing shoulders in the corner while they checked out the figures of the other attending guests.

On the men's side, I noticed my three friends from work, Ryan, Neil, and Dylan, plus Laura's husband Brad, Amy's boyfriend Lucas, the Brad Pitt lookalike Noah, the cute pizza delivery boy Alex, Paige's date Liam, and of course, Lincoln, with his big, beautiful, black cock. Standing in a separate corner chatting quietly with Madison was an intriguing new man, who reminded me of the handsome actor Patrick Dempsey from the television show Grey's Anatomy. I grabbed a glass of white wine from the kitchen island and sashayed up to Madison, winking at her playfully.

"You've got a bigger crowd than usual," I said, smiling at the new guy. "Word must be getting around about your stim-ulating parties."

"Possibly," she said, nodding toward her partner. "But I like to keep them on an invitation-only basis, unless we attract the wrong elements. I don't believe you've met my new boyfriend, Ben."

"Pleased to meet you, Ben," I said, shaking his hand softly. "Glad to see Maddy is beginning to widen her hori-zons. Does this mean the two of you will be *participating* in the festivities tonight?"

"I'm not sure what to expect," Ben said, peering at Madison with a furrowed brow. "I have to admit, this set-up looks a bit scary."

"You're in for a treat, then," I smiled, bumping the side of

Madison's hips. "Because Maddy's parties are always a hoot. I expect you'll be getting to know the rest of the group quite a bit more *intimately* before we're finished tonight."

"Speaking of," Madison said, peering around the room at the buzzing crowd. "It looks like everyone's arrived. I suppose I should get started explaining how this is going to work."

She strolled to the center of the room and tapped the side of her wineglass with a fork to get everyone's attention.

"Thank you all for coming to another one of my special parties," she grinned. "I know I was a little coy in my invitation regarding what I had planned, but those of you who've been to my previous events know that's half the fun. Not knowing who you'll be paired with or what you'll be asked to do makes it all the more interesting."

"True," Brad said, motioning toward the holes in the curtain. "Although the theme of this one doesn't seem quite as mysterious."

Madison nodded her head while everybody giggled.

"Yes," she said. "I suppose you can guess what those are for, but what you *won't* be able to guess is how I'll be arranging you to participate in the fun. I've cut a hole on each side of the curtain and four random participants will stand on each side while I select one person to stand on the opposite side..."

"I'm guessing we won't just be *standing* while we face one another, will we?" Mia chuckled.

"That's kind of up to you," Maddy said with a sly grin. "Depending on the manner in which you choose to engage with your partner."

"And by *engage*, I assume you don't mean with all of our clothes on?" Laura said, glancing at her husband's crotch, which was already beginning to tent outward in anticipation of the coming activities.

"Well, I suppose you *could*, but what would be the fun in that?" Maddy said.

"And these pairings will also be random in terms of *sex and gender*?" Shae asked.

"Absolutely," Madison nodded. "Although to keep it interesting, I'll be mixing up the pairings from round to round to build the excitement. By the end of the evening, hopefully all of you will have broadened your horizons in terms of potential connections."

"What if some of us aren't comfortable engaging in same-sex connections?" Lucas said, peering awkwardly at his girlfriend, Amy.

"Nobody will force you to do anything you don't want to do," Madison said. "That's part of the reason we'll have groups of four standing on each side of the curtain. If for some reason one of you doesn't feel like participating, I'm pretty sure there will be another interested participant ready to step up. Mind you, given the *size* of the hole in the curtain, you probably won't even know who's attending to your needs from the other side."

"And by *needs*, you're just not referring to the usual social niceties?" Dylan said, raising an eyebrow.

"I suppose that depends on what kind of *niceties* you're accustomed to," Maddy smiled. "I have a feeling that by the time we get through the first couple of rounds, your needs will be quickly expanding–"

"It looks like that's not the *only* thing that's expanding," I chuckled, motioning toward the bulging crotches of most of the men.

"I'm glad to see some of you are already starting to get

warmed up," Madison grinned. "That will definitely help us get off to a running start."

She glanced around the group, nodding her head while she tapped her finger softly in the air.

"To arrange our initial pairings," she said, "I'd like each of the men to count themselves off starting with the number one. Then each of the women will do the same, beginning with the number eleven. But don't forget to remember your number, because I'll be grouping you by number."

Everybody glanced at one another with a confused expression, then Madison pointed at Ryan to get the numbering started, nodding her head gently towards him.

"One?" Ryan said tentatively.

"Two..." Neil said after Madison pointed at him next.

After the last man counted to ten, Madison then pointed toward Lily, nodding her head to keep it going.

"Eleven..." Lily said, followed by the rest of the women until the entire group was divided equally into two groups of ten.

"Alright," Madison nodded. "Now I want those persons with numbers one and eleven, plus two and twelve, to shift to the side of the curtain nearest the fireplace.

Lily, Ryan, Bonnie, and Neil slowly shuffled their position as Madison had instructed, then she called out the next sequence of four to take up positions on the other sides of the curtain until there were only eight of us left.

"Now I'd like those with numbers seventeen through twenty to move to the *final* side of the curtain," Madison said.

Shae, Paige, the new girl, and I glanced at one another with a confused expression, then we peered back at Madison with pinched eyebrows.

"Why are the other groups *mixed,* but ours is comprised only of women?" I said, shaking my head.

"Because the last group of men will be going *inside* the curtain," Madison smiled.

She raised one side of the drape and motioned for Alex, Ben, Lucas, and Lincoln to step inside.

"What do you want us to do once we get in there?" Ben said, peering at Madison with a puzzled expression.

"For now, I just want each of you to strip down naked. I'll tell you what to do next in a minute."

Her boyfriend paused for a moment, shaking his head uncomfortably.

"Are you sure you're okay with me mixing it up with the other guests this way?" he said.

"I'm *more* than okay with it," Maddy grinned, winking toward me. "And I'm pretty sure it won't take long for *you* to be okay with it too."

After the men disappeared inside the tent, Madison turned toward the four women remaining on our side of the curtain, then she paused until the sound of rustling clothes stopped inside the cube.

"Are you boys ready in there?" she called from outside.

"If by ready, you mean *naked*, then yes," Lucas chuckled.

"Good," Madison said. "Now, I want each of you to walk toward one side of the curtain and stick your willies through the hole."

There was an awkward pause from the other side of the curtain, then one of the men cleared his throat.

"What if we're...um...partially *aroused* already?" Lincoln said.

"All the *better*," Madison smiled.

When I saw one of the men's half-erect dicks poke through the curtain on our side, I was a little disappointed it wasn't Lincoln's big black tool, but it was nevertheless still fair-sized, and rapidly rising. I had no idea which of the other three men it belonged to, but that was part of the excitement. Neither person on either side of the curtain would know who they would be engaging with, and my panties were already beginning to moisten imagining all the possible permutations.

"Excellent," Madison nodded, admiring the upturned pole of the contestant on our side of the curtain. "Now, for this *first* round, we're going to start off somewhat slow and easy. I'm going to ask one person from the opposite side of the curtain to step forward and manually stimulate your partner's penis with your hands only."

"Only *one*?" Paige smiled.

"For now, yes," Madison said.

"Does it have to be a *girl*?" Laura said from the opposite side of the cube.

"Absolutely *not*," Madison replied. "That's half the fun with this game. Besides not knowing who your partner will be on the opposite side of the curtain, you *also* won't know what sex or gender they are."

She paused for a moment while she darted her eyes across the faces of the women in my group, then she smiled.

"Are you guys ready to get started?" she said.

"Judging by the angle of our partners' cocks, I'd have to say that's a *yes*," Shae chuckled.

"Alright then," Madison smiled. "Let's get the party started."

Ready for more erotic chills and thrills? To read the rest of this story, click here:

GLORY
HOLE
AN EROTIC PARTY GAME
VICTORIA RUSH

ALSO BY VICTORIA RUSH

Adult Fairytales:

The Enchanted Forest: An Erotic Fairytale

The Land of Giants: An Erotic Fairytale

The Dragon's Lair: An Erotic Fairytale

Witch's Brew: An Erotic Fairytale

The Mage's Spell: An Erotic Fairytale

The Mermaid Lagoon: An Erotic Fairytale

The Coven: An Erotic Fairytale

Rapunzel: An Erotic Fairytale

The Seven Dwarfs: An Erotic Fairytale

The Land of Mutants: An Erotic Fairytale

The Erotic Temple: A Sexy Fairytale (Coming Soon)

Erotica Themed Bundles:

Voyeur: Lesbian Erotica Bundle

Public Affairs: A Lesbian Anthology

Futa Fantasies: The Ladyboy Collection

Threesomes: The Lesbian Collection

Threesomes - Volume 2: The Lesbian Collection

First Time: A Lesbian Anthology

Hedonism: An Erotic Anthology

Switch Hitters: Bisexual Erotica

Taboo Erotica: The Lesbian Series

BDSM: The Lesbian Collection

Party Games: The Erotic Collection

Party Games 2: The Erotic Collection

All Girl 1: Lesbian Erotica Bundle

All Girl 2: Lesbian Erotica Bundle

All Girl 3: Lesbian Erotica Bundle

All Girl 4: Lesbian Erotica Bundle

Erotic Fairytale Bundles:

Clover's Fantasy Adventures: Books 1 - 5

Clover's Fantasy Adventures: Books 6 - 10

Erotic Fantasy:

Pirate's Bounty: A Time Travel Adventure

Wild West: A Time Travel Adventure

Private Riley: A Time Travel Adventure

Cleopatra's Secret: A Time Travel Adventure

Bounty Hunter 2125: A Time Travel Adventure

Ninja Assassin: A Time Travel Adventure

The 300: A Time Travel Adventure

Arabian Nights: An Erotic Fairytale (coming soon…)

Steamy Time Travel Bundles:

Riley's Time Travel Adventures: Books 1 - 5

Lesbian Erotica:

The Dinner Party: Lesbian Voyeur Erotica

The Darkroom: Bisexual Voyeur Erotica

Naked Yoga: Lesbian Transgender Erotica

Nude Cruise: Bisexual Voyeur Erotica

Rush Hour: Taboo Public Sex

The Girl Next Door: First Time Lesbian Erotic Romance

Girls' Camp: Lesbian Group Sex

Wet Dream: Ladyboy Fantasy Erotica

The Convent: Taboo Sex with a Nun

Sex Robot: A Dream Sex Machine

The Personal Trainer: Getting Pumped at the Gym

The Dominatrix: BDSM Lesbian Domination

Webcam Chat: Lesbian Online Sex

Paint Me: A Kinky Bodypainting Workshop

The Toy Party: Girls Sharing Sex Toys

The Costume Party: Strapping One On

Swedish Sauna: Lesbian Group Sex

The Therapist: Taboo Lesbian Erotica

Elevator Shaft: Bisexual Threesomes Erotica

Ladyboy: Lesbian Transgender Erotica

Peep Show: Lesbian Voyeur Erotica

The Dare: Public Sex Erotica

Maid Service: Lesbian Threesomes Erotica

The Hitchhiker: First Time Lesbian Erotica

The Housesitter: Spycam Lesbian Erotica

The Spa: Lesbian Group Orgy

Parlor Games: Blindfold Sex Party

The Exchange Student: First Time Lesbian Erotica

The Hostel: Bisexual Group Erotica

The Harem: Lesbian Erotic Romance

The Orient Express: Lesbian Voyeur Erotica

The First Lady: A Forbidden Lesbian Erotic Romance

The Slave: Lesbian BDSM Erotica

The Masseuse: Lesbian Sensuous Erotica

Too Close for Comfort: Lesbian Forbidden Erotica

Naked Twister: A Wild Party Game

Lexi: The Sex App (Lesbian Fantasy Erotica)

Call Girl: Lesbian Bisexual Threesomes Erotica

Circle Jill: Lesbian Masturbation Workshop

The Viewing Room: Masturbation Voyeur Erotica

Spin the Bottle: A Kinky Party Game

The Hair Salon: Lesbian Voyeur Erotica

Tribadism 1: Girls Only Sex Workshop

Tribadism 2: The Art of Scissoring

Tribadism 3: Threeway Hookups

The Kiss: A Game of Oral Sex

Pledge Week: Sorority Sisters

Carny Games 1: A Wild Sex Party

Carny Games 2: A Kinky Sex Party

Carny Games 3: An Erotic Sex Party

Dreamscape: An Artificial Reality Game

Glory Hole: Guess Who's On the Other Side

Joy Ride: A Late Night Erotic Bus Trip

The Blind Girl: An Erotic Romance(Coming Soon)

Lesbian Erotica Bundles:

Jade's Erotic Adventures: Books 1 - 5

Jade's Erotic Adventures: Books 6 - 10

Jade's Erotic Adventures: Books 11 - 15

Jade's Erotic Adventures: Books 16 - 20

Jade's Erotic Adventures: Books 21 - 25

Jade's Erotic Adventures: Books 26 - 30

The Costume Party: Strapping One On

Swedish Sauna: Lesbian Group Sex

The Therapist: Taboo Lesbian Erotica

Elevator Shaft: Bisexual Threesomes Erotica

Ladyboy: Lesbian Transgender Erotica

Peep Show: Lesbian Voyeur Erotica

The Dare: Public Sex Erotica

Maid Service: Lesbian Threesomes Erotica

The Hitchhiker: First Time Lesbian Erotica

The Housesitter: Spycam Lesbian Erotica

The Spa: Lesbian Group Orgy

Parlor Games: Blindfold Sex Party

The Exchange Student: First Time Lesbian Erotica

The Hostel: Bisexual Group Erotica

The Harem: Lesbian Erotic Romance

The Orient Express: Lesbian Voyeur Erotica

The First Lady: A Forbidden Lesbian Erotic Romance

The Slave: Lesbian BDSM Erotica

The Masseuse: Lesbian Sensuous Erotica

Too Close for Comfort: Lesbian Forbidden Erotica

Naked Twister: A Wild Party Game

Lexi: The Sex App (Lesbian Fantasy Erotica)

Call Girl: Lesbian Bisexual Threesomes Erotica

Circle Jill: Lesbian Masturbation Workshop

The Viewing Room: Masturbation Voyeur Erotica

Spin the Bottle: A Kinky Party Game

The Hair Salon: Lesbian Voyeur Erotica

Tribadism 1: Girls Only Sex Workshop

Tribadism 2: The Art of Scissoring

Tribadism 3: Threeway Hookups

The Kiss: A Game of Oral Sex

Pledge Week: Sorority Sisters

Carny Games 1: A Wild Sex Party

Carny Games 2: A Kinky Sex Party

Carny Games 3: An Erotic Sex Party

Dreamscape: An Artificial Reality Game

Glory Hole: Guess Who's On the Other Side

Joy Ride: A Late Night Erotic Bus Trip

The Blind Girl: An Erotic Romance(Coming Soon)

Lesbian Erotica Bundles:

Jade's Erotic Adventures: Books 1 - 5

Jade's Erotic Adventures: Books 6 - 10

Jade's Erotic Adventures: Books 11 - 15

Jade's Erotic Adventures: Books 16 - 20

Jade's Erotic Adventures: Books 21 - 25

Jade's Erotic Adventures: Books 26 - 30

Jade's Erotic Adventures: Books 31 - 35

Jade's Erotic Adventures: Books 36 - 40

Jade's Erotic Adventures: Books 41 - 45

Jade's Erotic Adventures: Books 46 - 50

Fifty Shades of Jade: Superbundle

Standalone Stories:

The Polynesian Girl: A Lesbian EroticRomance

FOLLOW VICTORIA RUSH:

Want to keep informed of my latest erotic book releases? Sign up for my newsletter and receive a FREE bonus book:

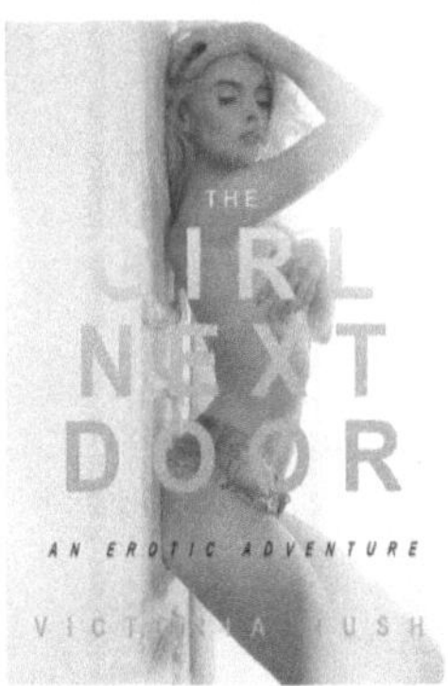

Spying on the neighbors just got a lot more interesting...